A LANDSLIDE, A BRIDE
AND A FATAL RIDE

Shiraz Jones Marine Rescue Mysteries
Book Three

*Dedicated to Lindsay Stenniken,
a Marine Rescue Volunteer whose experiences inspired
some of the storyline.*

Copyright

A Landslide, a Bride and a Fatal Ride:
Shiraz Jones Marine Rescue Mysteries Book Three

ISBN: 978-0-6451187-9-7
Imprint: The Cozy Cabin Press
10 9 8 7 6 5 4 3 2 1

CONTENTS

Shiraz Jones Marine Rescue Mysteries are set in England and written by an English author.

They may contain 98% less instances of the letter 'z' than competing products.

CHAPTER ONE

April 2nd, 1976

They came for him at dawn.

Three sharp raps on the blue, rotten-around-the-edges, wooden door which served as the entrance to his remote, stone cottage.

He didn't sleep much, so he was already awake.

And he'd been expecting them.

Expecting them for five weeks, six days and seven hours.

He lay motionless on his back, as a further three taps echoed around the flagstone-floored hall downstairs.

"Patrick." The voice yelled up to his bedroom window. "Come out. We know you're in there. Open the door."

Cold sweat ran down his forehead. They'd already called twice, and he couldn't ignore their summons forever.

"Come on, Patrick. Don't make us break it down. It's no use hiding."

His eyes stared at the ceiling, as the spring sunrise glowed orange through the curtains. He weighed up his three options. None of them were appealing.

He could simply stroll downstairs in his dressing gown, open the front door and accept his fate. They'd secure him, take him away, and he might never taste fresh air again.

Not his preferred choice.

He could pretend he wasn't home. Or hide in the secret cupboard. The one he'd discovered in the eaves, behind the old coats, spiders' webs and boxes.

No.

They'd find him eventually. He couldn't stay concealed forever.

Three thumps with a fist.

"Patrick. Open the door. Last chance."

Third option it was.

He wiggled onto his front, extended his arm and reached for the shotgun.

CHAPTER TWO

Present day

"Fire! Fire. Fire. Fire in the port engine. Mayday! Mayday."

Emily and I froze. My mind shuffled through scenarios we'd rehearsed in a desperate attempt to identify if this was one of them.

"Splintering shipwrecks." Murph stood with his clenched fists planted on his hips. "If this was real, we might have seconds to extinguish the blaze before our boat burns to the waterline. Shall we start again?"

My old life as the trophy arm candy of a London celebrity public relations guru lay over my shoulder. Ten weeks into my training with Redcliff Volunteer Marine Rescue, and I was messing up every drill. Together with Emily, my new best friend, I'd started my qualified crew education under the tutelage of Murph, the tall, broad, bald, bushy-bearded coxswain. We'd learnt about tides and first aid, safety gear and search patterns. He'd taught us what the various flashing lights at sea meant, and how to call for help in Morse code, which had proved to be very useful.

We'd completed five duties on board the primary rescue vessel, plus two unscheduled trips when he'd saved me at night from deserted beaches.

In both cases, I'd been entangled in two separate murder investigations, which certainly wasn't in my plan. You wouldn't move to a quaint, old seaside town and expect people to start dropping dead, would you? I mean, this wasn't some crime-ridden inner-city ghetto. This was safe, comfortable, Redcliff-upon-Sea, the little fishing port where I'd spent many happy childhood holidays playing on the beach with my parents and Poppy, my Corgi.

The marine rescue volunteers had fascinated me then. Brave men, dressed in waterproofs, answering rocket flares in the middle of the night, launching their vessel to save poor wretches in peril somewhere out on the ocean. I'd watched them from my bedroom window as their boat zipped towards the horizon, and I'd silently prayed for those men to return safely. So when I left my vapid, meaningless city life behind, I determined I'd make a difference. And in the enlightened days of the 2020s, there was nothing to stop ladies signing up to help save lives at sea. Even five-foot-ten ladies who were more accustomed to wearing high heels and figure-hugging dresses than bright-yellow waterproofs.

But now the boat had caught fire. Another of Murph's surprise assessments.

"Shiraz, Emily, gather round." Murph pulled out the *Redcliff Volunteer Marine Rescue Workbook* and opened it to a page in the middle. "In the event of a fire in the engines, what do we have on board to extinguish it?" He held the workbook open and turned it towards us.

Emily raised her hand. "Fire extinguisher? Dry chemical powder? Used for class A, B and E fires."

"Maybe," said Murph. "And well done for remembering the fire classes. You've been studying."

Emily swept her blonde bob back with a quick movement and looked jolly pleased with herself. I wasn't sure I'd even read this page yet.

"Which class of fire would a boat engine be, Shiraz?" asked Murph.

"Um, B?"

"Very good," said Murph. "You've been studying too. What's actually burning in a B-class fire?"

Oh great. I haven't studied this at all. If the boat engine's alight, B might mean boat?

"Does the B stand for boat?"

Murph shook his head. "Dislocated Daggerboards. B does not stand for boat. Have another guess."

"It's fuel," whispered Emily. "Petrol, for instance."

"Petrol," I said.

Since when did 'B' stand for petrol?

"Correct," said Murph. "Well prompted, Emily. However, we carry a more suitable item than an extinguisher for putting out an engine fire. Any ideas? It's in the workbook." He closed the book, so we couldn't cheat.

Emily shrugged. I shook my head.

Murph turned to a man who'd stepped out of the wheelhouse to join us. "David, please put these recruits out of their misery."

David, butcher by trade, marine rescue superstar by reputation and, when I'd first arrived here, potential boyfriend material. He was considerably younger than my thirty-eight years, but I was in great shape and could pass for thirty. David was definitely too young for me, I'd concluded. Maturity in a man was so attractive. Although maybe not quite as mature as my former husband, PR guru to the stars, Monty Jones. He'd tipped the age scales at almost seventy.

Emily and David had also shown interest in each other, and I wondered if their relationship would be one of those where both parties are mutually attracted, but they never successfully do anything about it.

"We carry a fire blanket," said David. "In the event of a blaze in the engines, a blanket soaked in sea water thrown over the fire will deny it oxygen far quicker than an extinguisher."

"Exactly," said Murph. "Shall we practise that again?"

A crackling sounded from the cabin. "Marine Rescue Redcliff, this is Coastguard Headland Bay. Come in, please. Over."

Phew. Saved by the radio.

David ducked his head through the cabin door and grabbed the handset. "Coastguard Headland Bay, this is Marine Rescue Redcliff receiving. Over."

"Please proceed to Golden Beach. We closed it because of a large landslip last week, but a member of the public reported a person and a dog stranded. Perform a welfare check and assist if necessary. Over."

"Marine Rescue Redcliff proceeding to Golden Beach. We'll call you when on scene. Over."

"Thank you. Coastguard Headland Bay out."

Murph closed the workbook. "We'll come back to our fire drill after we've dealt with this." He took up position behind the wheel and pushed the throttles forward gently. "Everyone holding on?"

"Holding on," we responded.

The tone of the engine changed. David punched buttons on the navigation screen, while I glanced over his shoulder.

"Golden Beach has super-unstable cliffs," he shouted above the noise of our powerful twin outboard engines. "The land there's always slipping. I've heard, in the 1970s, there was a road along the clifftop between Redcliff and Headland Bay via Golden Beach, lined with rows of wooden houses. But, little by little, the land's slipped into the sea, and hundreds of feet of coastline have been lost. All those homes are long gone, and the road too. Now anyone driving from Redcliff to Headland Bay has to divert miles inland via Alnchurch."

"Gosh," I said, "I didn't realise the cliffs were so precarious."

"The biggest slip was in 1976," added Murph. "Valentine's Day. We're quite accustomed to winter storms, but this one was exceptional. Even though I was only six years old, I clearly remember the night. I lay awake, terrified my bedroom would blow into the sea. We lost slates from our roof, trees blew over, and the river flooded so high, all kinds of things washed away. My mum took me on a walk around the town the following morning. As a small boy, watching the fire brigade pump out homes excited me, but thinking back, it must've been devastating for the occupants. My uncle's house flooded to the first floor; he found his motorbike swept down the river and onto the beach."

I visualised the quiet brook flowing through Redcliff's town centre and tried to imagine it as a raging torrent capable of transporting a motorbike.

We held on as the rescue vessel turned to starboard and rounded a promontory. Spray covered the boat's windscreen as we bounced over the waves, and my knees rode the swell like a snow skier riding the crests.

"My dad led the relief effort at Golden Beach," continued Murph. "The emergency services were fully employed helping people in Redcliff itself, and Dad knew Golden Beach Village would be isolated and in big trouble. He gathered men and women from the town, and they formed a rescue party. With no social media in those days, he assembled them simply by banging on their doors. At first light, the group drove along the cliff road towards Headland Bay in any vehicles they could find. Cars, bikes, several people rode in the back of Tommy Colstead's truck. When they reached Golden Beach, a scene of complete devastation greeted them. Houses had dropped over the cliff, cars were on their sides and the road had completely gone. Where the route to Headland Bay used to be, there was now a giant bite taken out of the land. And on the other side of it, you could see the road continuing. Of course, that's all disappeared over the years as the cliffs continued collapsing. Nothing remains of the road now."

"I think my dad was involved too," said Emily. "I wasn't born in 1976, but you've triggered a memory of something he said when I was younger. He told me they saved almost everyone."

"They did," said Murph. "They crawled down the cliffs among the houses, all jumbled up and collapsed like a smashed construction kit. People were trapped, calling out for help. None of those brave men and women had any search and rescue training, yet they saved over fifty souls. It made the national news. The Valentine's Day hurricane. You can read all about that terrible night at the Redcliff Museum. Have you been there yet, Shiraz?"

"I haven't," I said. "Where is it?"

"In the town hall, under the clock tower."

Murph pulled the throttles back and slowed the engines as we came within sight of a wide expanse of shingle. Exactly in the centre, a fan shape of red earth cascaded down from a scar on the cliff face. Tiny figures stood at the top and gazed over the precipice.

David pointed. "Those rubberneckers are risking their lives. Fifty feet of land's fallen into the sea, and they're standing on the edge and gawping at it. More cliff could easily slip away and take them with it." He grabbed binoculars and lifted them to his eyes.

"I can see someone on the beach." I pointed ahead and to the left.

David swung his gaze towards the far side of the landslip. "One person and a dog. Exactly as Coastguard said. Murph, can we get close enough to wade in?"

"Definitely. There are no rocks here, just shingle. You won't need to take a swim."

He idled the engine until we reached the shore, then I heard the clanking of the anchor chain and a motor whirring as the engine stopped. He raised the propellers clear of the water.

"Three feet of water under us," said Murph. "You can paddle. Take Shiraz with you. Give her experience of recovering people from the beach. She should know what it feels like to be on the other side of a rescue."

I bristled at Murph's subtle jibe.

David jumped overboard in his dry suit, held out his hand to help me, and we waded through the shallows together.

"Afternoon, sir," he called to a scruffily dressed man standing on the beach. His mongrel barked at us, and the man yelled at it.

"Are you hurt at all?" I called.

"No. Cold and wet." The man coughed continually, a deep, phlegmy sound, and his accent surprised me. It reminded me of a street trader in London's East End. I wondered why he wore heavy-rimmed sunglasses on this overcast day.

"What are you doing here?" asked David. "The beach is closed because of the landslip." He waved his arm towards the sluice of rocks and red earth.

"Rebel ran under the fence, and I had to chase after him." He nodded at the dog and coughed again. "He's a terror for sprinting off and won't come back when I call."

"You were lucky there wasn't another slip. These cliffs are unstable," I said, glancing at David to see if my local knowledge impressed him.

The scruffy man coughed again. "Sorry, Officer. I'm not familiar with this beach. I'm here on holiday."

I smiled at him. "There's no need to call me 'Officer'. We're marine rescue volunteers, not law enforcement."

"You're safe now," said David. "We'll take you back to Redcliff. Sorry, sir, this'll be undignified. Could you put your arm around my neck? I'll pick you up, and we'll wade out to the boat."

"What about Rebel?" asked the man. He pointed at the short, stocky animal, who definitely had Staffordshire Bull Terrier genes, and who wouldn't shut up.

"Shiraz'll carry Rebel. You'll both be safe."

"Quiet, Rebel," said the man. "This nice lady'll look after you."

Oh, great. Rebel doesn't look like he wants to be friends.

David lifted the scruffy man through the shallows, and I approached the dog, who backed away from me and growled.

I reached my arms towards it. "Here, Rebel. Good boy."

Rebel didn't want to be a good boy. Despite his diminutive size, this animal had a big dog bark on him.

"Come on, Rebel. Easy does it."

As I touched his collar with one hand, he turned tail and ran towards the back of the beach.

Great. I'm dressed in a dry suit which makes me look like a big, yellow astronaut, and now I'm tasked with chasing across a shingle beach after a dog. Who's probably going to bite me.

Rebel, of course, thought this was a great new game. Far from being in the slightest bit concerned a complete stranger had abducted his master and carried him out to sea, Rebel believed his mission in life was to lead me in a race up the beach, among the knots of black seaweed and the dunes of shingle.

I clomped after him in my heavy waterproofs, calling his name, which he didn't seem to know. Several times, he'd turn to face me and tip his head on one side with his tongue lolling happily. Each time I reached him, he'd sprint off again, and I couldn't believe a little animal with six-inch-long legs could run so much faster than I could.

I wondered what he'd do once we reached the back of the beach, under the cliffs where the landslip covered the grey, shiny, pebbles.

He paused, turned back towards me and then headed up the pile of red earth.

I performed a quick risk assessment. Should I pursue him across the landslip, which might be unstable and dangerous? Or should I abandon the chase, turn around and hope he followed me? Rebel crested an incline, then halted and barked repeatedly, and I could see the constant wagging of his short, brown tail. Against my better judgement, I climbed the landslip, reached the point where he'd stopped, and grabbed his collar.

Gotcha.

It was then I discovered what had distracted him.

In a dip, where the landslip had ripped away from the cliffs, among trees and bushes uprooted by the earth movements, I glimpsed something which definitely didn't belong there. The sight took me back to my teenage years, and my older cousin proudly displaying his new purchase.

Half buried in the mud.

Dented and broken.

Covered in rust.

The upside down, rear end of a sports car.

CHAPTER THREE

"Shiraz, what are you doing up there?" David's voice called from the beach. "You shouldn't be on the slip."

"Coming. I've caught the dog." I pulled out my phone, snapped two quick photos of the rusty car and picked up Rebel, who was remarkably heavy for his size. He wriggled in my arms, and I slid down the pile of earth ungracefully on my backside.

"Here," I said to David, shoving the dog into his arms. "You carry him. He's very solid." I turned around to gaze back up the landslip, but I couldn't see the spot where I'd been.

We trudged back to the sea.

"Why were you up there?" asked David.

"Fetching the dog, of course."

"We have to be careful under the cliffs, Shiraz. You know that. This section of coast's dangerous." He waved his arm towards the landslip. "Your life's more important than someone's dog."

"Um, the earth felt firm there. I didn't feel myself sinking. And you told the man I'd look after his pet." I didn't appreciate his lecture.

We waded to the rescue vessel, climbed on board via the ladder, and David handed Rebel to his owner. Murph pushed the throttles forward and pointed the boat's bow towards Redcliff.

I leant away from the scruffy man. Downstream of his body odour wasn't a pleasant place to be, and I didn't know if his persistent cough was catching.

"Emily, d'you know anyone who owned a blue, 1970s Mark IV Triumph Spitfire?" I stared at my phone and zoomed in and out with two forefingers.

We were in the apartment above her café, where I pretended to help in return for accommodation. I wasn't the most qualified kitchen hand, as I'd employed a personal chef during my former life in London, and Emily had given up on me ever learning to slice a tomato. Or load a dishwasher. Or make a toasted sandwich.

She poured us a second glass of opaque, blackcurrant-coloured Cabernet Sauvignon, took a sip and rolled it around her mouth. "Anyone in Redcliff-upon-Sea, d'you mean?"

"Redcliff, or, more specifically, Golden Beach."

"Nobody lives in Golden Beach."

"No, but they did before the Valentine's Day cliff collapse in the '70s."

"Shiraz, you're making no sense at all. Why would you want to know who owned a blue Triumph Spitfire in the 1970s and lived in a town which isn't a town anymore? And more to the point, why d'you think I'd know the answer?"

"You've lived here all your life. I thought you might remember something."

Boots, the Redcliff Marine Rescue communal ginger cat, stretched across her sheepskin rug until he was almost three feet long from toe tip to tail. He yawned, turned over and returned to his slumbers. I paused, sipped wine and lifted one eyebrow.

"Uh-oh," said Emily. "I know that look. The last time I saw that expression on your face, we ended up investigating a murder. What's inside that pretty head of yours?"

"When we were out on the rescue boat today, saving the man and his dog…"

"…which looked like it'd bite your head off, then dashed away?"

"Correct. When I eventually grabbed it, halfway up the landslip, I noticed the slip had carried a car over the edge. It was lying upside down, half buried in the earth."

"Maybe somebody parked on the cliff to look at the view, and drove too close? Or"—she pursed her lips and squinted—"maybe it was stolen? Someone took it for a joyride, then shoved it over? There are teenagers around here who'd be stupid enough."

"I suppose either of those scenarios is possible. Except the car looked as if it'd been buried for years. I took a couple of photos." I rotated my phone and showed her.

"Gosh, yes. It is filthy. How can you be sure it's a Triumph Spitfire? Specifically, a Mark IV? All I can see is the rear end."

"My older cousin owned that model when I was a teenager. He took me for a ride, and I remember that was the first time I'd been in a car without adults; I couldn't stop grinning. Maybe it's his old car? There can't be many blue Mark IV Triumph Spitfires."

"Could be. I don't recognise it. But we know someone who might."

"We do?"

"Yep. Oscar Wainwright."

"Of course. Let's track him down tomorrow."

The following morning, we discovered Oscar tidying Redcliff Marine Rescue's gift shop.

"Morning, Oscar. Are you opening for the season?"

Cadbury, his enthusiastic chocolate Labrador, jumped up to greet us.

"Morning, Shiraz. Morning, Emily. Is the café not open today?"

"It's Sunday. Day off."

"Ah, yes, of course. I'm tidying and dusting before the Easter school holidays. It's not worth opening before then; there's not enough passing trade."

I glanced around at the shelves stacked with tea towels, bookmarks, mugs and keyrings, all decorated with the marine rescue logo or with images of the rescue boat. One shelf displayed picture books with photographs of vessels. I picked one up and flicked through it, as Oscar opened a cardboard box and unpacked calendars.

"D'you have anyone to help in the shop?" I asked.

"Yes, in the summer. That's the busiest time; July and August. The rest of the year I can manage by myself. It keeps me fit in my retirement. Along with my daily exercise and sea swimming with the Redcliff Icebergers. Sometimes, customers want to chat about my time as a marine rescue skipper and quiz me about any exciting experiences. I enjoy the reminiscing and hope there are no other shoppers at the same time to interrupt me."

We laughed.

"A man came in yesterday morning as I was unpacking this new stock. A scruffy chap with a dog. Cadbury growled at the animal, which is most unlike him, so I asked the man to leave his dog outside." Oscar lowered his voice. "I encountered people like him during my police career. I reckon he was a rough sleeper. You have to feel sorry for these people. He smelt like he hadn't washed for a long time."

Emily looked at me. "That must be the chap we picked up yesterday."

"It sounds like him," I said. "Did he wear big, heavy-rimmed sunglasses? And was the dog called Rebel?"

"I didn't hear the dog's name," said Oscar, "but the man wore sunglasses inside, which I thought odd. And he coughed continually. We don't see many people like him in Redcliff-upon-Sea."

"What questions was he asking?"

"Very specific ones. Considering his appearance, he seemed to be well informed. He wanted to know about Redcliff Marine Rescue's role in the 1976 Valentine's Day landslip which wiped out Golden Beach Village."

"Really? Because if it's the same chap, we found him on Golden Beach yesterday afternoon."

Oscar set down the box he was unpacking. "There's a coincidence. And as an ex-policeman, I don't like coincidences. What was he doing there? It's closed, isn't it, because of last week's new cliff collapse?"

"Yep. A member of the public rang the Coastguard to say they'd seen him there, and they radioed us to pick him up. I chased his dog all around the beach; the silly animal didn't want to be rescued. It led me up on the landslip."

"David wasn't too impressed with you following it," interrupted Emily. "I think he felt responsible for you."

My face reddened. "Annoyed at me, you mean. Maybe I shouldn't have run up the landslip, but how else would I fetch the dog? Anyway, halfway up, the dog stopped and, once I reached it, I found the back end of a car, upside down, buried in the ground. I took a picture, and Emily thought you might recognise it." I unlocked my phone, swiped to find the image and showed it to Oscar.

"Gosh. It looks like it's been underground for a while." He tugged his spectacles down his nose. "It's hard to tell what make of car it is."

"It's a blue Mark IV Triumph Spitfire," I said. "My cousin owned the same model in the same colour when I was a teenager."

"Can you zoom in?" asked Oscar. "On the number plate?"

I spread my forefingers across the screen and showed him again.

"The first letter might be a 'Y'," he said, "but it's covered in dirt and bent over at the end so we can't see what the rest says. D'you have any other photos?"

"One of the side. The front of the car's completely buried."

Oscar inspected the second photo. "All we can tell for certain is it's a dirty-blue old car."

Emily peeked around Oscar and stared at the image on my phone. "This car must've been caught up in the 1976 landslip, completely buried, then partially revealed in the new earth movement last week."

"The timeline fits with your theory," said Oscar. "It's a shame the number plate's not visible. We might find out more if we had that information."

"Yep," said Emily. "This is one mystery we might never solve. Would either of you like lunch? I have café leftovers which need to be eaten."

"Not for me, thanks," said Oscar. "My wife and I are invited to a church Sunday roast. I don't mind going to church for the food. I'm not so keen on the sermon."

We laughed.

"Mmm, I love Sunday roast," I said. "Especially beef with crunchy Yorkshire puddings. What are you offering, Emily?"

"Chicken wraps? And if you're lucky, cream puffs for dessert."

"Count me in," I said. "We'll see you later, Oscar." I patted Cadbury as we left.

Emily unravelled the cling film around the wraps, sliced them in half diagonally and laid them on two plates. I eyed the cross section her knife had revealed and licked my lips at the exposed crunchy salad. Boots realised chicken was on offer and rubbed himself around her legs, miaowing constantly.

"All right, Boots. Enough." Emily laughed. "I'll give you chicken from my wrap. Here." She dropped two pieces of cooked meat into a bowl and placed it on the kitchen floor.

I boiled the kettle and brewed tea. "That Valentine's Day landslip must've been some event. An entire village dropped over the cliff, and fifty people homeless. Thank goodness for Murph's dad, and your dad, and everyone involved in the rescue effort. I'll visit the museum during the week and learn more about the event."

We sat at her table, and I sipped my tea.

"I can see cogs turning in your mind," said Emily. "Penny for your thoughts."

I laughed once. "D'you own a spade?"

"What, like a bucket and spade? The souvenir shop on the High Street sells them."

"Not a kids' toy. I mean a spade for digging gardens."

"I might do. My father was a keen vegetable gardener, and I still have his tools. They'll be under a cloth at the back of the garage. What did you want it for?"

"I'd like to take another look at the half-buried car."

"Shiraz, you're completely nuts." Emily's tea spilt as she crashed her cup onto the table, which made Boots jump a foot in the air and scrabble off across the floor. "I know you haven't lived here as long as me, but surely you understand how unstable those cliffs are? The new landslip happened just last week, and the beach is closed for a reason."

"Where the car was buried seemed firm enough. I, um, quite like trying to solve a puzzle."

"We're not talking about Sudoku. If you're only taking a look, why d'you need a spade?"

"Just in case, I suppose."

"Shiraz, stop staring at me like that. The last time I followed you on one of your wild duck chases along the beach, Marine Rescue took us home with our tails between our legs."

"Wild goose chases, Emily. And the tide won't cut us off this time."

"Us? What d'you mean, us? I'm not going with you. If you want to be buried under several tons of red earth on Golden Beach, you're on your own."

CHAPTER FOUR

"Emily, could you park the car any closer? The spade and shovel are awkward to carry."

"I can't believe I let you talk me into this. I said I'm only giving you a ride to the cliffs above Golden Beach. That's it. I'm not doing anything else. I'm dropping you in the car park."

"Please? You're here now. Could you drive across the grass to the Coastguard tape?"

"Shiraz, you're the absolute limit. This Morris Minor isn't an off-road vehicle."

"Could you help me carry the tools, then?"

"I'll bring the spade for you. But I'm not doing any digging with it."

Emily parked, and we marched along the cliff path above Golden Beach. A stiff breeze sliced through me, and I was glad for my super-warm, red, Moncler ski jacket. Emily had discovered a garden spade among her father's old tools, and I'd also come across a pointy shovel, which resembled something a gravedigger might use. At the edge of the landslip, a giant-sized bite had been dumped in a delta shape over the shingle below.

Waves crashed against the invading soil, and uprooted trees washed into the sea.

Emily pointed at a warning tape around the rock fall. "The name's a clue. Safety barrier. We're not supposed to go past it. Why are you so fascinated by this old car, anyway?"

"To see the number plate. I want to see if it's my cousin's. His was stolen years ago, and he'd be overjoyed if we found it." I lifted the tape, which broadcast in orange letters, 'COASTGUARD. DANGER. DO NOT CROSS', and held out my arm, inviting her to duck under it.

Emily shook her head. "If the emergency services knew what we're doing, they'd have us arrested." She followed me under the tape.

"Now what?" she asked, as we peered over the edge to where the earth had slumped across the beach.

"Now we climb down onto the landslip."

"Uh-uh. Now *you* climb down onto the landslip. I stay here so, when you get into difficulty, someone can call for help."

"I'm not getting into difficulty. I'll have you know, at Thornhill Grange Private Ladies' College I excelled in outdoor education. Mountaineering, orienteering, abseiling. Once, we were alone on the moors for two nights as part of survival training. Just because I wear Dolce and Gabbana doesn't mean I can't be rough and tough when I want to be."

"But we don't have any mountaineering or abseiling equipment. Dolce and Gabbana or otherwise."

"Dolce and Gabbana don't make mountaineering equipment, Emily. We'll improvise." I grabbed hold of an uprooted tree and slid down the first section of landslip on my bottom. Suddenly, I wasn't sure about this exercise, but I couldn't let Emily know my doubts. I turned around and shouted up to her. "Could you throw the spade, please?"

"What if I hit you with it?"

"Okay, don't throw it. Slide it down to me."

Emily leant over the edge of the cliff and dropped the spade. I grabbed it and stuck its blade into the soil.

"Now the shovel."

Emily reached behind her for the shovel. As she dangled it over the edge, the soil crumbled beneath her, and she slid feet first on her bottom, tobogganing down the landslip towards me and screaming as she approached. I grabbed her as she careered past, and she knocked my legs out from under me. We tumbled further until a bush arrested our descent.

We froze and stared into each other's eyes.

Emily's voice shook. "What happened?"

"Um, you decided to join my little adventure, after all?"

She pushed herself onto her knees and glanced above us. "I knew I shouldn't have listened to you. Now we're halfway down a landslip which could collapse further at any minute, and there's no way we'll ever be able to climb back up again." She sat and held her head in her hands. "This is all a bad dream. I'll wake up and I'll be back in my café, and you and your crazy schemes won't be part of my life anymore."

"Calm down, calm down." I pushed myself to my feet and brushed dirt from my clothes. "We have a job to do." I grabbed the spade and inched myself towards the half-buried car. "Come on, Emily. I need your help."

The upside down car hadn't moved from where I'd seen it on Saturday, which at least showed the cliff hadn't collapsed further.

"So this is your car," said Emily. "I never realised exhausts were so big. All you see normally is the little tube sticking out at the back, but miles of pipes under the car are hidden."

I wiped mud from the rear. "I knew it," I said, as I revealed the word 'Spitfire' in metallic silver.

"And look," said Emily, digging in the mud, "I've exposed the whole number plate."

"Well done," I said. "See, we make a great team." I rubbed dirt from the plate with my hands. "It's one of those old-fashioned licence plates where the letters and numbers are screwed on. Not printed like these days. Oh. It's not my cousin's car. I remember his registration had seven digits. This only has five. There's a 'J' and a 'Y' and a '4'. There are also two spots with screw holes, but the letters or numbers are missing. So it's J-space-Y-4-space."

Emily laughed. "This is like doing the Wordle."

"I'm glad to see a smile on your face."

"It doesn't mean I'm any less annoyed with you for dumping us in this pickle."

"We're here now. Can you help me dig out the front of the car?"

"Why? You've discovered it's not your cousin's."

"Clues, Emily, clues. It shouldn't be here. We should discover as much about it as we can." I dug more soil away. "If we can see inside, we might work out why it's been buried."

Emily sighed. "Why do I feel we're getting involved in a mystery again? Life was so easy until you came along." She rolled her eyes and began to shovel.

The loose earth came away easily and, within ten minutes, we'd uncovered the underside of the vehicle, open to the elements in its upside down position.

Emily wiped her brow with her sleeve and transferred red mud to her face. "Now what?" she asked.

"Now we dig around the driver's door. I can see the top edge. I suppose it's the bottom edge, really, as the car's upside down." I stuck the pointy shovel against the car and scooped. Emily helped me and, little by little, the driver's door was revealed. The bonnet and passenger side remained buried.

"Can you see in the car yet?" asked Emily.

"It's full of sticks and dirt. Hang on." I tugged a twig from the driver's seat, which snapped off and exposed half the steering wheel.

I sat down and puffed. "This is hard work, Emily. Grab this big branch with me."

We grasped limbs of the bush.

"It's coming," I said. "One, two, three, pull. And again. One, two, three, pull. I felt it move. One, two, three..." The branch dislodged, and we fell over backwards.

Emily looked at me. "Hah. You should see the state you're in. You need a bath."

"So do you. You're covered in earth."

She laughed. "I always wanted red hair. But I didn't mean like this."

We stood and wiped the earth off ourselves, then Emily stuck her head into the upside down car, pulled it out and looked away.

"Emily, are you okay? What's wrong? Why have you turned white?"

She covered her mouth with her hand and shook her head slowly. "Look...inside...the...car. But only if you have a strong stomach." She bent over, held her knees and panted.

I frowned, crouched and peered past the steering wheel into the passenger seat.

A human skull stared back at me.

CHAPTER FIVE

I squeezed my eyes closed and clenched my teeth. "I've never seen human remains, and I didn't think I would today."

"Me neither. Now what do we do?" Emily glanced back at the car but didn't dare look inside again.

"I know exactly what we do. Call the emergency services and tell them we're on the landslip at Golden Beach and we've found a body."

Emily puffed hard. "We're in so much trouble. Why do I ever listen to you?"

"Emergency. Which service?"

"Coastguard."

"What's your location?"

"Golden Beach."

"Golden Beach, near Redcliff-upon-Sea?"

"Correct. There are two of us, and we're stuck on a landslip." I didn't expand about the skeleton.

"Your name, please?"

"Shiraz Jones."

"Please wait, caller."

I heard a dial tone, then a third voice.

"Coastguard Headland Bay."

"Emergency operator connecting mobile 07700 900119."

"Your reference CGHB-78311. Go ahead, caller."

"Um, hi. Could you please send help to Golden Beach? We need police and ambulance as well. Actually, don't worry about the ambulance. It may be a bit late for medical help."

"What's the nature of your emergency?"

"We're stuck on a landslip."

"How many people are stuck?"

"There are two of us, um, three really."

"Your names?"

"Shiraz Jones and Emily Philpot."

"And the third name?"

"I don't know."

"Okay. Are any of you injured?"

"No, but one of us is dead."

"A member of your party has died?"

"Um, they weren't with us when they died. They've been dead a long time. Decades, possibly." This conversation wasn't playing out quite the way I'd planned.

"Please clarify the situation," said the Coastguard operator. "Two people are stuck on the landslip at Golden Beach, alive and well. Yes?"

"Yes."

"And you have a dead body with you?"

"Yes. We've found a dead body. Inside a car."

"Are you certain they're dead?"

"I'm trained in first aid, and I can confirm this person is well beyond benefiting from any medical treatment. They're a skeleton."

"I see. Okay, stay where you are. We'll send a rescue team to you. Call us again if the situation changes. And I'll ring the police about your discovery. We'll be with you in thirty minutes or less."

"Thanks. See you soon." I sat upwind of the car. Emily crouched next to me, hugged herself and shook her head.

"Shiraz Jones, if anyone had said to me this morning I'd be tumbling down a landslide and sitting with a skeleton waiting for the emergency services, I'd have told them they were completely nuts. What are you getting me into this time?"

I wrapped my arm around her and smeared mud over her coat. "Life's never boring since you met me, is it?"

"Hello? Anyone down there? This is the police."

A deep, slow, country voice called from the cliff above. I stood, turned around and stared up into the evening light.

Emily pushed herself to her feet. "That sounds like Constable Bert." She shouted. "Bert. It's Emily and Shiraz. We're here. Halfway down the landslip."

A younger, more directive voice. "Stay where you are. The Coastguard's on their way."

"Constable Lachlan," said Emily to me. "The young policeman. Oscar doesn't rate him. He says he thinks he knows everything."

"Are you both all right?" asked Bert's voice. "No bumps or bruises?"

"We're covered in mud," I called back. "No injuries."

"You shouldn't be down there." Lachlan's voice. "This area's closed for your own safety."

"Now, now, Lachlan." Bert's voice. "Let's rescue the ladies first and worry about how they got into this muddle later."

"But, Bert, we can't rescue them and pretend they haven't done anything wrong."

"We'll deal with that later. Look, here come the Coastguard four-wheel-drive vehicles. Wave your arms to direct them to the scene; there's a good lad."

Although we couldn't see what was happening thirty feet above us, I smiled to myself at Bert and Lachlan's different approaches to community policing.

Emily grabbed my arm. "What are we going to tell them about why we're here? We can't say we didn't see the safety barrier."

I thought for a moment. "We'll say we were out for an afternoon walk, and we noticed the car from the clifftop. As we're both trained in first aid, we jumped down to the crash site, not in the slightest bit concerned for our own personal safety, to see if the driver needed help."

Emily held her palm to her heart. "Shiraz, you're such a quick thinker. Oh. How do we explain the spade and shovel?"

"We'll say we'd just finished gardening, which is why they were in your car. We grabbed them in case we needed to dig anyone out of the car."

"But I don't have a garden."

"Um, we were digging for fishing bait in the sand?"

"I don't go fishing."

"Oh, for goodness' sake. I'll think of something."

Another voice from above us. "Hello. Is everyone all right? This is the Coastguard. Can you see me?" I looked up and observed a head wearing a white helmet poking over the edge of the cliff.

"Yes. We're here." I waved my arm.

"Everyone okay? No broken bones?"

"No bones broken. At least, Emily and I haven't broken anything."

"Stay there. We'll come down to you."

Emily bent her head to me. "When do we tell them about the skeleton?"

"Leave that to me. We need the Coastguard to witness the body in the car and then tell the police. It'll sound better coming from them."

"Lower!"

We heard a shout from above, and a red rope appeared over the cliff edge. A figure in blue overalls made his way down the landslip backwards. He arrived at our position, unclipped the rope from his waist and shouted, "Safe!" then turned to us. "Hello, I'm Adam, a Coastguard rope technician. Nobody's hurt, are they? What are your names?"

I wondered how we both looked, dressed in filthy clothes, covered in mud, and our faces smeared in red dirt. Adam was a good-looking chap, and I would've preferred our first encounter to be in an expensive restaurant, when I was wearing a cocktail dress and heels after a trip to the hairdresser.

"I'm Shiraz, and this is Emily. We're both fine. A little cold."

Broad, tall and clean-shaven, with a rugby player's broken nose which only made him more attractive, Adam wore a medley of yellow straps around his overalls, and a radio hung from a belt around his waist. He switched his glance between Emily and me. "How did you end up down here? Did you fall?"

I pointed at the upside down Triumph Spitfire. "We were walking along the cliff enjoying the spring sunshine, when we glanced over the edge and saw this."

"You were walking along the cliff carrying spades?"

"Yes. We always do. In case we see any, um, molehills which need flattening."

Emily's eyebrows raised, and she mouthed, "Seriously?"

I whispered back, "You come up with something better."

Adam gave us an odd look, then glanced upward and made a thumbs up to a colleague above. I could see him puzzling how we'd glimpsed the car from the top, as it was still mostly buried.

"Anyway," I continued, "We're both medically trained, so without a thought for our own safety, we scrambled down to see if anyone in the car needed help."

"Medically trained?" asked Adam. "Are you doctors?"

"Um, no," said Emily. "First aid only. We're volunteers with Redcliff Marine Rescue."

I quite liked Adam thinking I was a doctor.

"Obviously you didn't find anyone in the car needing help?" he asked.

I sighed. "They're beyond help. Look."

Adam bent down as I crouched and pointed. I was torn between enjoying our proximity and trying not to be sick.

"Woah." He recoiled and stood. "Yep, they're definitely beyond help."

His pallor whitened, but he held it together.

"The first thing to do is get you two out of here. Then we'll tell the police about your discovery, and they can deal with it. That's not for us search and rescue crews, right?"

We're both search and rescue professionals. This is me, living my new life.

Adam continued. "The Coastguard helicopter's on another job. We could wait an hour for it to become available, but you both seem strong and fit. I reckon we'll manage without it. Have either of you done any rock climbing?"

"I haven't," said Emily. "Although earlier I did some rock sliding."

Adam laughed. "What about you, Shiraz?"

He got my name right first time. What a guy.

"I climbed at school when I was a teenager. But not since."

"This'll be considerably easier than any rock climbing you've done. We're going to walk up the slope where you two slid down, but this time, you'll be strapped to one of us." He spoke into his radio. "Adam to Jordan."

The radio crackled. "Receiving."

"Jordan, could you join us and bring two harnesses? The two people are fit and well, and we'll extract them by walking them back up the cliff."

A second rope dropped over the edge, and an identically uniformed, tall, stocky woman descended.

"Hi, ladies, I'm Jordan. Please don't worry. We'll have you out of here in no time."

The last thing I wanted was for Jordan or Adam to think we were incapable weaklings. I wanted to show I was as tough as she was.

"Thanks, Jordan. It's a little embarrassing; you guys rescuing us, seeing as we're fellow emergency search and rescue workers."

"Are you with Redcliff Marine Rescue?"

"We are."

"Gosh. They're going to have a good laugh at you about this, aren't they?"

It won't be the first time.

Adam turned to Jordan. "Don't look in the car."

"What car? Oh." Jordan noticed the inverted Triumph. "You two weren't in the car, were you?"

"No. It's a long story. I'll tell you at the top."

Adam took charge. "Let's harness you both up. This part goes over your head, then you slide your arms through here."

I enjoyed the closeness of him dressing me and made a mental note to make sure he helped me take my harness off at the top. Meanwhile, Jordan helped Emily into her straps.

Adam pointed at the first rope. "See this clip. We'll attach it to a hook on your belt." He tugged the silver carabiner around my waist, and I quite liked the action. "One of us will hold on to the rope, and we'll walk up together. You can't fall, because the clip only goes up, not down. If you need to rest, we'll stop. Jordan'll be right behind you." He pointed at Emily. "Emily, you and I will climb the other rope. We'll tie the spades to another line and pull them up separately. I want you to hold on with both hands."

The rope ascent made me feel like a spider walking up a wall. I crawled over the cliff edge at the top and sucked in a quick breath at the sight of around twenty people watching me, including two other Coastguard employees. The unintentional audience clapped and cheered as Jordan and Adam followed Emily and me.

"It looks like you two are quite the celebrities," said Constable Bert, removing his helmet and sweeping it in a gesture like a Shakespearian actor.

Adam helped us out of the harnesses as Officer Lachlan swiped open an iPhone and poised his forefinger over it. "Your full names, please?"

"Hang on, young lad," said Bert. "Let them recover from their ordeal. We'll take them back to the station for a cup of tea."

I took Bert's arm and guided him away, while the Coastguard team packed their vehicles. "Bert, there's something I need to tell you." I darted a glance over the cliff. "There's an upside down car on the landslip. And there's a body inside it."

CHAPTER SIX

"The Coastguard mentioned you said something about a body," said Bert. His cheeks puffed out.

"It looks like it's been there a long time."

"A dead body?"

"Yes, Bert. A dead body. A skeleton."

"Skeleton? It's definitely dead then?"

"Definitely."

"A dead skeleton." He removed his helmet again and scratched his head. Wisps of grey hair blew in the breeze as he glanced over the edge of the cliff. I briefly wondered how many live skeletons he'd come across.

"I'll call Sarge," he said. "He'll need to know about this."

Lachlan dispersed the crowd by making shooing motions and yelling as if he were herding sheep. "What's the hold up, Bert? We need to take these suspects to the station to interview them."

"Enough hollering, Lachlan, there's a good lad," called Bert. "And don't refer to members of the public as 'suspects'. Shiraz has something we need to tell Sarge."

Lachlan marched towards us. "I'll record her conversation as evidence." He brandished his iPhone again.

Bert wagged his finger. "Lachlan, make yourself useful and grab the police tape from the car. I'll call Sergeant Will."

Lachlan huffed, swivelled on his heels and strode back to the police vehicle. Emily chatted with Adam, Jordan and the other Coastguard technicians. Lachlan approached their group, no doubt to warn Emily under no circumstances was a dangerous criminal such as her to leave the scene without permission. Bert dialled and raised his phone to his cheek.

"Sarge? It's Bert. Yes, I know it's your day off, but this is important. D'you remember Shiraz and Emily from Redcliff Marine Rescue? They've found a body."

A pause, while Bert avoided my eyes.

"Yes, they're sure it's dead. No, I haven't seen it myself. Nor has Lachlan. But I don't have any reason to suspect they're unreliable witnesses."

I interrupted him. "The Coastguard man, Adam, he saw it too."

Bert continued talking into his phone. "We have Coastguard with us, Sarge, and they've also seen the body. Apparently, it's been dead some time. Decades, I think, from Shiraz's description."

He paused again, and I couldn't hear the other end of the conversation.

"Right-o, Sarge. We'll set up a crime scene and expect you shortly. I'll advise nobody to leave. Yes, I'll get names, addresses and phone numbers. Yes, I'll ensure no one disturbs evidence."

He scratched his head and spoke into the phone again. "I don't suppose you could pick up doughnuts on the way? Oh. Right. I guess not then. Bye, Sarge. See you shortly."

Bert replaced the receiver and pulled at his ear. "Sarge wants everybody to stay here until he arrives. It's his day off, so he wasn't in the best of moods. I was looking forward to my Sunday teatime doughnut."

"Sorry, Bert. Pop into Emily's café tomorrow, and we'll find something nice for you."

"You will?" He licked his lips. "I am particularly partial to her pastries, I must admit. Especially the ones with the gooey, oozy, chocolate filling. Nothing like them anywhere else, that's what I always say. The other day, I was out for tea in Headland Bay with the wife, and we ordered a cake from one of the cafés in the High Street. I remember saying to her, 'This is stale as toast. Nowhere near as good as Emily's'."

"I'm so glad you like them, Bert."

Lachlan appeared, waving a roll of blue-and-white tape. "Shall I roll this out, Bert?"

"I've spoken with Sarge," said Bert, "and this is now officially a crime scene." He puffed out his chest and inserted his thumbs in the lapels of his jacket.

Lachlan shook his head at him. "Then you should remember from your training that any bystanders are to be removed immediately." He made further sheep-ushering movements with his arms.

"None of your cheek, Lachlan. This is the real world, not the Police Training Academy. All in good time." He turned to me. "Shiraz, would you mind joining the others and remaining here while we secure the area?"

I frowned and drew my head back. "Are we under arrest?"

"Of course not, but we'd prefer it if you didn't leave."

"Aren't they the same thing?"

"I'm sure Lachlan could tell you the official answer from the police manual. I'm politely asking you to hang around for a bit."

I laughed. "Sorry, Bert. I'm only teasing."

Bert led me away while Lachlan made a few more sheep-directing motions and rolled out two lines of tape which repeatedly stated 'POLICE LINE DO NOT CROSS'. The barriers flapped in the breeze behind me as Bert and I joined Emily and the Coastguard employees.

"Sorry to detain you," said Bert, "but given the discovery which Shiraz and Emily have made, I need everyone to remain here until the sergeant arrives. While we're waiting, could I please make a note of names, addresses and phone numbers? We'll start with you, Shiraz."

Bert jotted down Emily and me as living above the Wicked Whelk café, and he made a note of our numbers. We looked up at the sound of a vehicle speeding down the gravel track towards us. A plume of light-brown dust blew from its rear.

"Here's Sergeant Will," said Bert. He turned towards the clifftop. "Lachlan, have you finished rolling out the tape?"

"I have secured the crime scene, yes, Bert," said Lachlan. He marched towards the car park and accosted the sergeant as soon as he opened his car door.

"Sarge, reporting I've secured the crime scene, and confirming all bystanders are clear of the area."

"Thank you, Constable." The sergeant stepped out of his green saloon and stood. He wore a diagonally chequered jumper, fawn trousers and white shoes. As he exited the vehicle, he rammed a brown, tweed, flat cap on his head. "I've interrupted a perfectly good game of golf with Grantley Bramhall to attend this scene. I was about to score a birdie on the ninth too." He turned to Bert. "Constable, what d'you have?"

Bert produced his notebook, which caused Lachlan to shake his head and begin scrolling his iPhone as if it contained important information.

"Shiraz and Emily here," Bert indicated the two of us, "had proceeded in a downwards direction onto the landslip…"

"…where they shouldn't have been," interjected Lachlan. "They crossed Coastguard tape illegally."

"Thank you, Constable. I've asked Bert to brief me," said the Sergeant. "And Bert, they didn't 'proceed in a downwards direction'. They went down."

Bert licked his pencil. "As I was saying, Shiraz and Emily were on the landslip, and they discovered an upside down car.

Upon investigating further, using spades they conveyed with them..."

"Why were they carrying spades?" asked Lachlan. "This seems very suspicious."

"We'll consider everything as we investigate," said the sergeant. "Please allow Bert to finish."

Bert shuffled his feet and harrumphed. "As I was saying, they investigated the upside down car using their spades and, in the front seat, they state they saw a dead body, to wit, one skeleton."

"And you mentioned the Coastguard rescue team witnessed the skeleton, too?"

"That is my understanding. I've taken all their names and addresses." He proudly held up his notes, written in neat, cursive pen.

The sergeant took the notebook and addressed us. "The Coastguard employees may leave the scene, but please, could you drop into Headland Bay police station to submit a report? I'm sure you know the procedure."

Adam hopped in the liveried off-road vehicle with his colleagues. He gave me a brief smile, and I blushed.

My coyness was interrupted by Sergeant Will. "Shiraz Jones and Emily Philpot, I'll need to ask you to accompany Bert and myself. We'll take a formal statement."

"What about my car?" asked Emily. She pointed at the Morris Minor which stood where she'd left it in the car park before our adventure had begun. Its light-blue paint had turned dusty brown from Sergeant Will's sudden arrival.

"You can drive your own vehicle, Miss Philpot. Don't go fleeing the scene. The last thing I want is to chase fugitives when I should get back to my game of golf." He turned to Lachlan. "Constable, please stand guard and keep onlookers away. I'll arrange for you to be relieved before dark."

Lachlan took up station in front of the police tape, standing rigid in a military pose with his hands clasped behind him and his back to the sea. I smiled to myself at how seriously he took his role.

As Emily folded down her car's convertible roof and placed the spades carefully in the back seat, I glanced back at the cliff edge.

I couldn't see the car anymore, but I could see the beach beyond.

I paused and shaded my eyes.

Was it a trick of the light, or had the scruffy man with the dog returned?

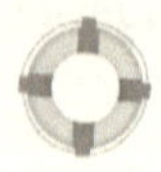

CHAPTER SEVEN

I took two steps forward and peered over the edge again.

"Ms Jones," called Sergeant Will. "I do hope you're not planning another foray down the cliff."

The figure had vanished. A dog barked, but the sound could've come from any direction.

"Sorry, Officer. I thought I saw someone, but I've decided I'm imagining things."

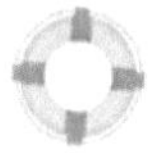

Sergeant Will showed us into an interview room which contained four chairs: two on either side of a white, Formica-topped table. He disappeared down the corridor, and Bert popped his head around the door.

"Tea?" he asked. "With a digestive biscuit? I'm sorry we can't provide the quality of Emily's catering."

"I'd love tea, thanks," said Emily. "And a biscuit."

"I don't suppose you could rustle up a double shot skinny latte, could you?" I asked.

Bert wrinkled his brow. "Is that a sort of coffee, Miss? We have instant granules."

"Never mind. I'll have a tea. Same as Emily. Thank you."

Bert gave us a thumbs up. "I'll leave the door open, so you know you're not incarcerated."

A kettle boiled in an adjacent room.

Emily folded her arms on the table and crashed her head onto them. "What have you got us into now, Shiraz Jones? Why, why, why did I listen to you? All I wanted to do this afternoon was put my feet up on the one day off I earn per week, maybe read my book or watch something on TV, and instead I find myself falling down a landslip, discovering a skeleton and ending up in the police station." She lifted her head and glared at me. "This is absolutely it, Shiraz. Next time you tell me we're off on some wild duck chase, you can leave me behind."

I decided not to correct her idiom and rubbed her shoulder. "I'm sorry, Emily. But I couldn't leave a half-buried car uninvestigated, could I?"

Emily clenched her teeth and glared at me. "Yes. Yes, you could. Or you could report it to the police, like any normal person would."

"Oh, Emily, where's the excitement in that?"

She puffed as Bert appeared with two mugs and a plate of biscuits. "Here we are, ladies. Sarge is on his way. Won't be a tic." He left the room and returned with two more mugs. Sergeant Will tailed him, carrying a pad and pen. His golfing outfit didn't match his official police demeanour.

The two policemen sat opposite us. Bert helped himself to a biscuit.

"Thank you for coming in, Ms Jones and Ms Philpot," said Sergeant Will.

Emily shrugged. "Did we have a choice?"

Will ignored her. "Ms Jones. Tell me about your discovery, from the beginning."

I explained how we'd been training on the marine rescue boat with Murph and David when we were asked to investigate the scruffy man with the dog on the beach. I told him about chasing Rebel up the landslip and finding the car.

"So why did you decide to return to the scene, armed with a spade and a shovel, and try to dig the car out? Why didn't you alert the authorities you'd found something unusual, instead of investigating yourself?"

"Exactly what I was thinking," Emily remarked. She blew out like a horse.

I didn't appreciate her siding with the police and ganging up on me. I could've done with some support. "Clearly I didn't realise we'd uncover a skeleton."

The thought of what I'd seen in the passenger seat made me shudder. "I merely wanted to look at the car as, when I was a girl, my cousin had the same model sports car which was stolen, and I wondered if it had turned up. That isn't something to bother the police or Coastguard about, is it?"

"Ms Jones, you crossed a Coastguard safety barrier. You must've realised it wasn't the right thing to do. You are, after all, involved in marine search and rescue yourself, aren't you?"

I thumped the table. "Could we focus on what's important here? If I hadn't crossed the tape and inspected the car, I wouldn't have found the body. The poor person's been buried for decades. My actions might bring closure for a grieving family who never knew what happened to their relative."

Sergeant Will pursed his lips and glanced away from me.

Bert blushed and cleared his throat. "Another digestive biscuit?" he asked, lifting the plate.

I shook my head once.

Sergeant Will continued. "Let's come to where you cross the Coastguard safety tape and scramble down the landslip."

"Tumble down, in my case," said Emily. "My backside still hurts, and I ripped my trousers. And could I point out I wasn't a willing participant in these shenanigans?"

Sergeant Will turned to her. "Who drove the car to the scene?"

"I did," said Emily, lowering her gaze. "But I didn't mean to get involved like this, did I, Shiraz?"

I bit my lip. "We descended the landslip and arrived at the point where I'd seen the car yesterday. The rear licence plate had numbers and letters missing, and I was interested in whether it was my cousin's car. I couldn't tell, so we started digging around the buried section to see if the front number plate was complete. It was then…"

Emily turned white.

"Are you quite all right, Miss Emily?" asked Bert. "Shall I fetch you a second cup of tea? Here, have another biscuit." He offered her the plate and helped himself to a digestive in the process.

Emily fanned herself and leant on me. "I'm sorry. I've never seen a skeleton. Except a cartoon one running after Shaggy and Scooby on *Scooby Doo*."

Even Sergeant Will managed to smile. "Let's stop for now. Take a break."

Emily panted and sat up. "Good. I need fresh air." She stood.

"I've called the body recovery team," said Sergeant Will, "and they'll be here tomorrow morning to complete the excavation you began." He gave me a wry look. "Please don't go anywhere near the scene again. No more investigating; leave that to us. Stay away from the cliffs."

"Definitely," I said. "Constable Lachlan wouldn't let me within a mile of the place."

Emily produced crackers and cheese for an evening snack at the little kitchen table in her flat, and I cracked open a bottle of Cabernet Sauvignon and poured two glasses. I sliced a wedge of Stilton, which crumbled and revealed its creamy, blue-veined interior.

"I'll only have one glass," said Emily. "I have to be up at five to open the café."

"Of course; it's Monday tomorrow. D'you need my help?"

"Um, no. Thank you."

"Great. I thought I'd take a walk around town. Maybe visit the museum, like Murph suggested. I'm interested in discovering more about the night Golden Beach Village disappeared over the cliff. He mentioned there was an exhibit about it."

Emily swirled her drink around in her glass. "I haven't been to the museum since a school excursion twenty years ago. It's silly, isn't it? You live somewhere and never visit the local attractions. Mind you, I can't imagine much will have changed. They'll still proudly display the moth-eaten dinosaur model and the toy soldiers."

We both laughed.

She sipped her wine. "And don't forget we have marine rescue training tomorrow evening. I wonder what Murph has in store for us this session?"

"Hopefully, some content I can remember?"

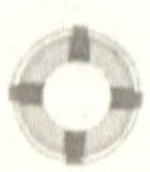

I woke the following morning to the sound of my bedroom window rattling, which it only did when there was a strong south-westerly wind. A tug at the curtains exposed a light-blue sky with fluffy, white clouds zooming across it. I tugged on my sneakers and slipped down the stairs. The front door nearly blew out of my hand, and I struggled to pull it closed again. Condensation ran down the windows of the Wicked Whelk café, as I nipped in to collect my regulation double shot skinny latte, without which my brain refused to function. Emily slipped me a cinnamon bun for breakfast, then I pulled my collar around my face and set off along the promenade, where waves whipped up by the gale bashed against the sea wall and sprayed white foam over me. I threw my head back and grinned, as the skin-awakening cold splashes stung my face, and I tasted salt. As I rounded the bay, I came across Oscar with his chocolate Labrador.

"Hi, Oscar. Hi, Cadbury." I rubbed Cadbury's head, and he rewarded me by shaking himself, spraying slobber in every direction.

"It's a blustery day for a walk, Shiraz," said Oscar. "Where are you off to?"

"A quick stroll around town, and then I thought I'd pop into the museum for something to do."

Oscar held one hand flat to the side of his mouth. "A little bird tells me you found a skeleton."

"How on earth did you discover that snippet?"

"Nothing gets past me in this town. Do tell me about it."

I sighed. "Emily and I revisited the old car I'd discovered in the landslip. We couldn't see the number plate, so we dug around in the loose soil to expose it. That's when we found the body in the front seat." I lowered my voice. "I'd never seen a dead body. Neither had Emily. But I'm willing to bet it's connected to the 1976 landslip, so I'm going to the museum to find out more."

Oscar glanced left and right, as if suspecting concealed spies might infiltrate our conversation. "Before you visit the museum, you may wish to take a stroll along the cliff path. The police recovery team's at work, and I understand they'll be lifting the car onto the clifftop today."

"But Sergeant Will told me to stay away."

"Did he now? What makes him think he can stop you from walking along a public footpath? It's not like you'll be crossing any police tape, will you?" He laughed.

"Um, no. I wouldn't dream of it." I winked.

Another laugh. "And when you've finished at Golden Beach and the museum, we should regroup. Because I have an inkling whose body you may've unearthed."

CHAPTER EIGHT

I gasped. "Seriously, Oscar? D'you know who was in the car?"

"I could take a good guess. Are you and Emily free this evening?"

"No, sorry. Marine rescue training tonight."

"You can't miss that, can you? Mustn't upset Murph."

"Sure. Um, could you tell me now whose body you think it is?"

"I'll let you piece together whatever you find today," he said, mysteriously, "and we'll see if we come to the same conclusion." He addressed Cadbury, who stood with his ears flapping, minutely watching a seagull peck at food packaging spilt from a rubbish bin. "Shall we keep going, Cadbury? We'll let Shiraz get on with her important investigations." He grinned and waved as they strolled off down the promenade.

I heard the police recovery team before I saw them. The walk along the cliff path from Redcliff-upon-Sea to Golden Beach had taken me the best part of an hour, even with the strong wind behind me and, as I marched up the bluff to the location of the landslip, the sound of a large-engined vehicle vibrated the air. A blue-and-white mobile crane had been parked close to the cliff edge. Three other police vehicles surrounded it, all the same model of car, all with a double cab and a large rear storage area. A flatbed truck completed the motley convoy. Men and women in dark-blue overalls carried equipment to and from the cliff edge and lowered it to unseen colleagues.

A rope cordon had replaced Lachlan's police tape, behind which a small crowd of around thirty onlookers gathered. As I approached, I observed one of them brandish a long-lensed camera, and he snapped photos of everything and everyone. I tugged my beanie hat over my ears in case the police recognised me, but neither Bert nor Lachlan, nor their sergeant were present to witness me disobeying their instructions to keep my distance.

The man with the camera turned to me as I joined the throng.

"Morning, Love," he said.

I didn't appreciate being called 'Love'. It reminded me of the way photographers addressed me when I posed with my husband for *Red Carpet Superstars* magazine. *Turn this way, Love. Give us a smile, Love. Hands on your hips, please, Love.* Urgh. I hated it.

"D'you know anything about this?" the camera owner continued.

"Not a thing." I decided to remain anonymous. "What's going on?"

"Apparently, yesterday, someone found a car which had fallen down the landslip." He lowered his voice. "Rumour has it, there's a body inside."

"Seriously?" I said. "Do we know who it is? Has anyone been reported missing?"

"That's what I'm here to find out." He held out his hand. "Roy Bartlett. Owner, publisher and reporter for the *Headland Bay Times*. The most popular local newspaper in the area."

"What d'you think happened?" I asked, feigning ignorance. "Did someone drive over the cliff? Maybe they had too much to drink?"

"If they had, they must've been blind drunk. The road finishes way behind us." He pointed over his shoulder with his thumb. "Ooh, quick. Get a load of this." He pushed between an elderly couple by almost climbing over the top of them, and I heard his camera click-click-click as two of the men in blue overalls appeared, carrying a long, black, zipped-up bag between them. They opened the rear of a vehicle and placed it carefully inside.

"Did you see that?" said Roy, turning to me triumphantly. "I was right. There was a body. I wonder who discovered the car here in the first place? I'll need an interview to go with the photos."

"I've no idea," I said, hiding my smile behind my lapels. "Maybe somebody spotted it from the clifftop."

The pitch of the crane's engine rose, and we heard it strain and rev. The noise steadied, and its long arm extended hydraulically. Above the edge of the cliff, the Triumph Spitfire came into sight on the end of the crane's chains, still upside down, suspended by a hook at each wheel. It was caked in the red earth, and twigs and leaves protruded from its undercarriage.

"Woah, check that out," said Roy. He machine-gunned photos as the swinging crane's arm deposited the car on the flatbed truck. Two police officers removed the chains and attached straps around the car's axles, tying it to the truck. They then covered it with a dark-grey tarpaulin and lashed it down tightly.

But before they did, I snapped a quick picture of my own.

The front number plate was visible, complete and, once I'd zoomed in, I could make out the registration.

J-O-Y 42.

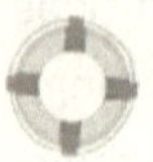

I'd never visited Redcliff Museum, despite having walked past it many times. Buried within the old town hall edifice, under the clock tower, I hadn't even realised it existed. I thought the building was merely a municipal office where people went to pay boring things like rates, which weren't relevant to me as I didn't own a house, or parking fines, also not relevant to me as I didn't possess a car. My pink, convertible Porsche had been owned by my husband's PR company, so when he went, so did my pride and joy. And now I was a marine rescue volunteer and not bimbo arm candy, I didn't miss driving one bit. To tell the truth, I'd always been nervous behind the wheel. I'd seen so many accidents in my rear view mirror.

The woman behind the museum counter glanced up at me over her half-moon glasses, secured to her neck by a gold-coloured chain. Her face reminded me of a bird of prey, thin and pointy with a hook nose.

She smiled. "Good morning. Welcome to Redcliff Museum. One adult?"

"Yes, please." I grinned and shrugged. "Just me. All alone."

She took the banknote I held and handed me my change. "It's lovely to see you, Miss. The Easter season's not yet upon us, so there aren't many visitors, and I've tidied the gift shop for the tenth time this week. Are you here on holiday?"

"No, I moved to Redcliff around two months ago. My name's Shiraz Jones. I live with Emily Philpot, above the Wicked Whelk café."

"How wonderful," she said. "We need more young people moving to town. Half the population are old fogeys, like me."

I smiled. "I'm sure you're not that old, Mrs...?"

"Farmer. Violet Farmer. And I'm nearly seventy." She laughed. "This part-time voluntary job keeps me young. Anyway, start in the room to your left and follow the arrows on the signs. Please ask me if you have any questions."

"Thank you. I will."

My sneakers squeaked across the shiny, parquet floor. The route around the museum was arranged chronologically, and the tour began in a room devoted to dinosaurs. I knew the land around Redcliff-upon-Sea was eroding and unstable but didn't realise it always had been. For millions of years, cliff collapses and landslides had changed the topography, and fossil hunters from around the world descended upon Redcliff whenever a new earth movement promised artefacts. I wondered if the homeless man with the scruffy dog was a fossil hunter, but he had none of the equipment, and his demeanour didn't suggest digging for prehistoric animal remains was his favourite pastime.

I paused in front of an exhibit describing the geology of the red cliffs which gave the town its name, seams of mineral-enriched rock stretching for miles along the coast. The corners of my mouth turned up at the sight of the moth-eaten T-Rex model illustrating the prehistoric era which, as Emily had suspected, no one had updated since her schooldays.

The second room in the museum displayed a life-size montage of primitive humans wearing animal skins, living in caves among the cliffs. It seemed contrived and probably based on an episode of *The Flintstones*, so I passed it by and wandered into the next room, where a display explained how the town of Redcliff-upon-Sea came to be sited where it was. It also informed me Redcliff Harbour was once one of the most important docks in the country and the site of a crucial battle in the 1500s which had changed the nation's history. A complicated skirmish had been laid out in 3D-detail as an aerial view, enacted by hundreds of badly painted toy soldiers. Emily's schoolday memory of the exhibit served her well.

On the wall hung a dramatic painting of a catastrophic storm which had occurred two hundred years later. The image depicted a three-masted sailing ship, clearly in mortal peril on the rocks, with people jumping from its decks into the raging sea, and others on the shore making desperate efforts to save them. The caption stated the storm had claimed over three hundred lives; the worst disaster in Redcliff's history.

After this time, Redcliff-upon-Sea had once again become a sleepy backwater, until Victorians discovered the medicinal properties of sea bathing and came in their droves from the cities. Old black-and-white photos showed bearded men wearing full-length bathing costumes, and women covered in frilly, head-to-toe outfits posing unsmilingly on what I could clearly recognise as Redcliff's Main Beach. I thought of my minuscule Seafolly bikini with which I planned to impress the natives this coming summer and smiled to myself as I imagined the horror this would've caused the people in the photo.

The next room in the museum depicted the history of Redcliff Marine Rescue. A sepia picture, dated 1880, showed men in front of an open boat on a trailer pulled by four black horses. The men had walrus moustaches, wore raincoats and sported primitive, cork lifejackets. I drew in a deep breath and felt a warm connectedness, as I acknowledged my role as a descendant of these brave people, a volunteer in the same tradition. Although I noted none of them sported a dark-brown ponytail or wore Chanel lipstick.

The last room contained information about Redcliff-upon-Sea today. I paused at a board which described the destruction of Golden Beach Village in the 1976 Valentine's Day storm and the accompanying landslip.

As Murph had outlined, a group of men and women from Redcliff headed three miles to Golden Beach along the old coast road at dawn on Sunday, February 15th, 1976. They took ropes, blankets, axes, sledgehammers; anything they could grab which might be needed. Off-duty nurses tended to the injuries of both those who had been made homeless and their rescuers. I did a double take as I read the names in the caption included Violet Farmer's, the woman working in the museum gift shop.

The photographs showed remains of smashed houses lying at the bottom of the cliff, and the caption stated the pictures were copyright of *The Redcliff and Golden Beach Herald*.

My eyes were drawn to a newspaper cutting dated February 5th, 1976, nine days prior to the storm. It showed a young man and woman standing in front of a row of terraced, red-brick houses. A tall, narrow, chimney featured prominently at the end of the street; the kind of view seen in northern mining areas, or factory towns. The couple's clothing suggested they'd been married the same day, and they didn't look comfortable in garments they clearly weren't accustomed to wearing. Whoever cropped the photo had chopped out the faces of people either side of the bride and groom. The caption stated, 'Patrick and Mary Hebblethwaite: two victims of the landslip still missing.'

I scrutinised the image. Time had faded the clipping, and the photo had been grainy to begin with. But directly behind the happy couple, at the end of a row of cars parked in the working-class street, decked out with ribbons and balloons, and with the words 'Just Married' graffitied across the rear, was a Triumph Spitfire.

And although the number plate was blurry, I was fairly sure I'd just seen the same one dangling from a crane.

CHAPTER NINE

I cleared my throat, so as not to sneak up and startle the woman in the gift shop.

"Hello, my dear," she said. "Did you find the museum interesting?"

"I did. Especially the part about the 1976 landslip. That was you, wasn't it, among the nurses who helped the survivors?"

"A much younger me, yes; how observant you are. What a terrible, terrible night." She shook her head slowly and gripped the counter. "My garden shed blew over, and I couldn't find my cat for days. I thought I'd never see him again, but the next week he waltzed back in as if nothing had happened."

"Poor puss. Um, could you tell me more about what happened at Golden Beach?"

Violet sat on a stool behind her cash register and sighed. "I came straight from work at the hospital when I heard about the disaster. An ambulance headed for Redcliff dropped me at the end of the clifftop road, then I walked the rest of the way. When I arrived, groups of people were sitting on the asphalt, dazed and confused. Some quick-thinking survivors had made a fire out of timber from a wrecked house, and people huddled around it to keep warm. I'll never forget the stench. It didn't smell like a fire you'd have at home. Men and women were digging in the wreckage with their bare hands, trying to pull people out."

Violet paused, removed her glasses and wiped her eyes. "Those brave people worked all day and rescued almost fifty inhabitants. Volunteers served tea and food and kept the homeless wrapped in blankets while I did what I could for the injured. We sent a young lad to cycle to Redcliff and fetch the ambulance for one old chap who'd been trapped under a beam when his house fell over the cliff. But the poor man died at the scene. Both Redcliff and Alnchurch ambulances were fully employed in their own towns, and the Headland Bay ambulances too. If anyone couldn't walk, we ferried them to the hospital in Tommy Colstead's truck. Mr Murphy, the man who led the rescue effort, received a medal for bravery, as did three others. He was, I remember, rather embarrassed by it. He felt everyone involved should've been recognised."

I wondered whether Murph still owned his father's medal.

"Apart from the poor old man under the beam, did anyone else die?"

"Three sisters who shared a house. The rescuers found their bodies under the debris. They didn't have a chance; I reckon their place was one of the first to tumble into the sea. And one or two people passed away in the hospital. But considering what had happened, it could've been worse."

"Yes, thanks to you and those other brave volunteers. What an amazing effort. Did they ever find the young couple in the newspaper cutting?"

"Who, dear?" She averted her eyes and fussed with souvenirs on the table in front of her.

"The ones in the paper. The wedding photo in your display."

"Oh, them. I can't remember. They'd recently moved to the area. No one knew them very well."

"Yes, I read that. Terrible. No closure for their families."

"No," said Violet. "Very sad. Anyway, it's been lovely to chat with you. Do pop in again."

"Bye, Violet. Nice to meet you."

I hurried out of the museum.

Two people unaccounted for, but it looked like their car had turned up in last week's new landslip.

And one of them might still be in it.

"Tangling turnbuckles," exclaimed Murph at Monday evening marine rescue training. "Why is modern technology so difficult to use?" He pressed his keyboard harder in the hope the action would persuade his laptop to do what he wanted, but to no avail.

His gaze swept over us new recruits. "Does anyone here know about computers?"

David, Murph's usual IT support, wasn't present, so I volunteered and walked to the front of the training room. I mean, I can work a smartphone. How much harder can a laptop be?

"What are you trying to do, Murph?"

"Make the laptop show this presentation on the screen behind us. I've connected the cable and pressed the button on the top row of the keyboard to share the screen like David showed me, but nothing's happening." He thumped the table and appeared to be about to throw the computer across the room.

"Did you turn the screen on?"

"Yes, the laptop's on." He jabbed his finger at the offending technology.

"Not that screen. The one behind you on the wall. Here." I pushed a remote control, and the television displayed its manufacturer's logo, then a red background with white words: 'Marine Rescue Academic Training part three'.

Murph hmphed. I grinned at him, set down the remote and rejoined Emily.

"All right, everyone." Murph's voice resonated around the room as he addressed the trainees. "During this week's session, we'll refresh what we know about fires. We'll revise the different types of fire and how to extinguish them, the most likely causes for fire at sea and then, during our practical training on the boat at the weekend, we'll run through another real-life simulation of an FOB, or Fire on Board." He pointed at me. "Shiraz, what would you think is the crucial difference between a fire on a boat in the harbour, and a fire on a boat out at sea? Don't worry if you don't know the answer, but have a guess."

"There's nowhere for survivors to escape to at sea."

"Correct. A boat fire out at sea is phenomenally dangerous, potentially fatal. There's nowhere for the crew and passengers to escape to, except into the water where they could drown. Anything else?"

Emily raised her hand. "It's harder to get help."

"Right," said Murph. "If a boat at sea catches fire, it can burn to the waterline as there are no resources nearby to extinguish it, such as a fire brigade, or water pumps. A boat on fire tied to a dock is in a much better position to summon help."

He continued with the presentation, which showed diagrams of different coloured fire extinguishers, complicated drawings which resembled physics experiments and cartoons of distressed people escaping burning buildings, cars and boats. I tried as hard as I could to concentrate, but my mind kept returning to the image of the body bag and the upside down car hanging from the crane.

"That ends this evening's academic session," said Murph, concluding a presentation which I hadn't taken notice of at all. "See you for boat training at the weekend. Remember to revise your workbooks, section four. Lastly, I've received your Redcliff Marine Rescue emergency service identification cards to hand out. And don't complain about the photos. They're the ones you gave us when you submitted your applications, but they always look funny on the cards."

Emily nudged me. "Let's go upstairs and grab a cup of tea and a biscuit before bedtime. I wish training finished earlier than nine-thirty on Mondays, with me having to open the café at six in the morning."

"Are you busy tomorrow after closing time, by any chance?"

"I don't have any plans beyond the usual food prepping and cleaning."

"If I help you with that, would you mind giving me a lift to Headland Bay? It's not far, is it?"

"No. Twenty minutes."

"So forty minutes if anyone else was driving?"

We both dissolved into giggles.

Emily nodded. "That's no problem. I can visit the wholesaler while we're there. Hey, show me your identity card photo. I'll bet it's even worse than mine."

I'd remembered to wear a headscarf to deal with Emily's insistence on having the convertible top lowered on her 1960s Morris Minor. Together with my Prada sunglasses, the look was very *Thelma and Louise*.

Emily accelerated out of Redcliff-upon-Sea along the inland road towards the town of Alnchurch, passing the turning to Redcliff Manor on our left, then the King's Arms pub on our right.

"What d'you need in Headland Bay?" she asked.

"There used to be a newspaper called the *Redcliff and Golden Beach Herald*, but I asked at the newsagent, and they said it ceased circulation years ago. The current local paper's the *Headland Bay Times*. They also said back issues of the *Herald* might be stored at Headland Bay Library."

"You're not getting us involved in another murder investigation, are you?"

"Whatever makes you think that?"

"I don't know, Shiraz. I have a funny feeling about whatever you're up to. How was your walk yesterday, and the museum?"

"Interesting." I turned my head to the side and gazed out of the passenger window.

"Interesting? Is that it?"

"The moth-eaten T-Rex and the toy soldiers from your schoolday excursions are still there, as you guessed."

Emily giggled. "Nothing's changed, then. But did you find out any more about the Valentine's Day landslip and the destruction of Golden Beach Village?"

"Yes, but..." I drummed my fingers on the dashboard.

"But what, Shiraz? Don't keep me in suspense."

She paused at the road junction in Alnchurch, indicated right and swept onto the main road to Headland Bay. I thought back to the era before Valentine's Day, 1976, when our journey would've taken the clifftop route before it was washed away.

"But now I have more questions than answers." I folded my hands and gazed into my lap.

"Go on," said Emily. "It's harder getting information from you than squeezing juice from a potato."

I forced out a breath. "Yesterday morning, while you were at work, I walked into town and bumped into Oscar. He'd heard about our discovery of the car and even knew it had a skeleton in it."

"Of course he had," said Emily, shrugging. "Where on earth does he get his information from?"

"No idea. He told me the police recovery team were removing the car as we spoke, and he suggested I stroll around the cliff to Golden Beach to watch them."

"But the sergeant told you to stay away."

"I know. Oops."

"Shiraz Jones, you are trouble. With a capital 'T'." She swerved onto the opposite side of the road to overtake a cyclist, and I held on and winced.

"Well?" continued Emily. "I presume you disobeyed police orders and visited the scene. What did you see there?"

"When I arrived, the police were busy. Although, thankfully, I didn't see any of the local police who would've recognised me. The recovery team extracted the skeleton in a body bag."

"Did you see it?"

"The body bag, yes. The skeleton, no. But we'd already seen that."

"Um, yes. We had."

"They had a giant crane on a truck, which they used to lift the car from the landslip, then they dropped it onto another flatbed vehicle and covered it with a tarpaulin.

But before they concealed it, I took a quick photo of the front; the part we hadn't been able to dig out." I wiggled my backside and tugged my phone from the pocket of my jeans. "Here's the picture." I showed her my screen, then wished I hadn't as she swerved across the road while inspecting it.

"Sorry, it's too small," said Emily. "What am I looking at?"

"D'you remember the rear number plate had missing numbers?"

"Yep. All we could find was a 'J', a 'Y' and a '4'."

"The front one's complete. You can see it in the picture." I enlarged the image with two forefingers but didn't try to show her again. "It says J-O-Y 42."

"J-O-Y 42? Joy for two? That's so romantic."

"Gosh, I never would've made the connection."

Emily slowed as we passed the speed restriction sign announcing the town of Headland Bay. "Did you see anything else at the scene? Or did Sergeant Will arrest you again?"

"You are funny. As Oscar said, they can hardly arrest me for walking along a public footpath, can they? But, no, after they'd secured the car on the truck, there wasn't any more action to watch, so I strolled back to town and dropped into the museum. After looking at the dinosaurs and soldiers, I discovered the exhibit about the storm and the rescue of almost the entire population of Golden Beach. In one of the newspaper cuttings from the time, there was a wedding photo of a young couple."

Emily slowed as we reached the town centre. "And?"

"And in the background, I think I saw J-O-Y 42."

"What, the blue Triumph?"

"Yep. The same one."

"Can you be sure?" Emily stopped outside a modern, single-storey facility one street back from the principal thoroughfare, with a sign saying, 'Headland Bay Library'.

"Nope. But I'm going to pop in here and find out." I opened the car door and stepped onto the pavement.

"What are you getting us into now, Shiraz?" Emily shook her head as she engaged first gear. "Call me when you're done, and you want to go home again." She indicated, and the Morris Minor pulled away.

CHAPTER TEN

I perused the shelves while waiting for the young, square-spectacled librarian to serve customers, then approached him once he was free.

"Hi, I understand you may have the records of a defunct local newspaper here, the *Redcliff and Golden Beach Herald*. I was hoping to inspect them."

"We do." He opened a metal filing cabinet behind him and tugged out a piece of A4-sized paper. "Fill in document request D11, then come back to see me. Next, please."

I accepted the form and sat at a desk to complete it. It asked for my full name, address and phone number, then details of the records I wished to study and my reasons for wanting to view them. I wrote 'family research'. This wasn't a complete untruth; I just wasn't researching my own family. I removed the pen from the paper and ran my finger down the checklist of items.

As I stood to return to the desk, someone touched my arm.

"Excuse me."

I swivelled to find an old man in a raincoat. He held a walking stick in his right hand and gripped my forearm in his left.

"May I help you?" I asked. I recoiled and tried to tug my arm away.

The man cleared his throat. "I overheard you asking about local newspapers. What did you need to know? Many years ago, I was a reporter."

I took a step back, and he released me.

"Were you a reporter for the *Redcliff and Golden Beach Herald*?"

"Young lady, I wasn't *a* reporter for them; I was *the* reporter. From the 1960s through to 1980, when the paper folded into the *Headland Bay Times*. They already had three staff, so they didn't need me, and I lost my job. If that cowboy Roy Bartlett had kept me on, his paper would've thrived, instead of becoming the free distribution rag it is now, with more estate agents' adverts than editorial. I'll have you know; I was the one who broke the story about the match-rigging scandal at Redcliff Rugby Club. The biggest piece of investigative journalism the paper ever published. Of course, there was the bigger story they didn't publish, but…"

"Excuse me. My phone's ringing." I unzipped my handbag and tugged out my device, desperately hoping I'd be able to press the green button before the sixth ring. "Hello? Hi, Emily. Okay, see you here in five minutes. Bye."

"I'm terribly sorry; I have to go. My friend's picking me up. It's been lovely to meet you, Mr…?"

"Leonard. Bill Leonard. As I was saying, the massive story the *Redcliff and Golden Beach Herald* never published was my investigation into the aftermath of the landslip." He wagged a long, bony finger at me. "I knew I had a gripping story there, but I couldn't gather enough evidence, and the editor refused to publish my findings. Pompous idiot. If he'd printed my article, we would've gone national. I reckon I could've got a book deal. Maybe even a movie. But it was a long time ago, and nobody's interested now."

My eyes opened wide. "Landslip? D'you mean the 1976 Valentine's Day landslip which destroyed the settlement of Golden Beach?"

"Of course I do. Which other one would I be referring to?"

"Um, I understand this part of the coast moves all the time; there are always bits dropping into the sea."

"That's as may be, but the Valentine's Day landslip's the only one with a secret."

"What secret would that be, Mr Leonard?"

My phone rang again. "Are you coming?" said Emily's voice. "I'm outside."

"Hang on, Emily. Two minutes." I turned back to Bill. "My friend's waiting for me. Could you give me your mobile phone number? I want to hear your story."

He laughed. "I don't own one of those new-fangled things. But if you want to find me, I'm here every afternoon, reading the newspapers. I'm glad someone's interested in my tale. No one was when it was important."

"My name's Shiraz. I'll pop back one day this week to buy you a coffee, and you can tell me about it."

"That's kind of you. It's been a long time since I've had anyone to share a coffee with. As I've said to my doctor many times, there should be a pill to combat loneliness in the elderly. Why, this morning, I woke up and realised I hadn't spoken to a soul, one on one, for almost a week. I enjoy a good chat; I rarely have the opportunity to nowadays, what with…"

"I'm so sorry, Mr Leonard. I'll drop this form at the counter; then I must head off. But I promise I'll be back another day."

My phone rang again as I joined the queue to see the librarian.

"Where are you?" said Emily's voice. "I can't wait forever. I'm parked illegally."

"Sorry; there's a lIne for the desk. Got to go. They're serving me." I pressed 'end' on the phone and turned to the young librarian.

"Here's the form D11. Is that everything you need?"

He scanned the paper. "I'll need to check you've completed it correctly. Do you have identification, please?"

I handed him my shiny new marine rescue card. He held it up and compared it to the form.

"Is Shiraz your first name, or your last name?"

"My first name is Shiraz. Jones is my last name." I pointed at the form. "I have filled it in correctly."

"And your address is the Wicked Whelk café, Redcliff-upon-Sea?"

"Yes."

"You live in a café?"

"I live above a café. Temporarily."

"I see. And your phone number is...?"

"...as written on the sheet."

"And you want to view the microfilms of the *Redcliff and Golden Beach Herald* for February 1976?"

I clenched my jaw. "Yes. That's what I've put on the form."

He handed me back my identification. "It'll be a couple of days. Please return after Thursday."

"I will. Anything else?"

The librarian desperately tried to find another minuscule detail to quiz me about. "No, I think that'll be all. Next, please."

Emily revved the engine as I opened the passenger door. "Where've you been? There's a traffic warden coming." She pointed up the road.

"Sorry. I was talking to a man." I lifted a cardboard box labelled 'butter' from the front seat, jumped in and rested it on my lap. As soon as I slammed the door, Emily accelerated away from the kerb as fast as the Morris Minor would go.

She shook her head at me. "Here I am, waiting forever, risking a parking ticket, and you're chatting up blokes?"

"I wasn't chatting him up. He was about eighty years old."

"Not much older than your last husband, from what you've told me."

"Very funny. Although, I am meeting him for a coffee on Thursday."

"I knew it," she said. "Is he a billionaire about to drop off the perch?"

"By the look of him, he's anything but a billionaire. But I want to pick his brains. He was the reporter who wrote the editorial in Redcliff Museum about the missing couple, plus unpublished pieces about the Valentine's Day destruction of Golden Beach. One of his articles which was never printed tells a secret about the landslip. I'm willing to bet it's something to do with the body in the car, so I'm going back to the library on Thursday to view the microfilms. And he told me he'd be there. He sits there every afternoon reading the newspapers. He's lonely, poor chap."

Emily shook her head and puffed. "Shiraz, what are you getting involved in? Neither of us were born in 1976. Some things need to be left to lie."

"No. I want to dig beneath the surface of this mystery, if you'll pardon the pun. We don't know who the person in the car was, and their family might be looking for closure on a relative who's been missing for decades."

"But why are you the one putting all this together? Shouldn't the police do that?"

I shrugged. "Maybe they will. Although, I doubt it. Because, right now, all they have is a skeleton in a car, which was probably buried in a landslip nearly fifty years ago. Whereas I might've made a connection as to who it is, and I want to hear this reporter's story. I reckon there could be more to this than another accidental death in the 1976 storm."

I glanced sideways at her, and she clenched her teeth.

"Why do I feel I'm tagging along on another of your investigations?"

"Um, because I'll need a ride back to Headland Bay on Thursday?"

"Sorry, I can't take you on Thursday. I have a dentist's appointment. There's a bus once a day. It leaves Redcliff-upon-Sea around lunchtime and returns in the late afternoon."

"Okay, that'd work. Brrr. My leg's getting cold from this carton of butter. Could I swap it for the box marked 'flour'?"

Oscar greeted us as we ferried Emily's groceries into the café.

"Hello, Shiraz, hello, Emily. Do you need a hand carrying those?"

Emily nodded. "Thanks, Oscar. There are a couple more to come from the back seat. Would you like a cup of tea? I've fresh scones from this morning which won't keep."

"I'd love a tea and scone, thanks. Plus"—he nodded at me—"I want to hear what you've been up to since we chatted yesterday. I may have some information which'll interest you."

"I knew it," said Emily, rolling her eyes. "We're putting the band back together."

Once we'd emptied the car, Emily produced three cups of tea and a plate of home-made scones served with red, oozing strawberry jam and a bowl of clotted cream which I spooned out in satisfyingly thick dollops. We sat around a table in the café and negotiated the division of five scones between three people as politely as possible.

"So, Oscar, what d'you have to tell us?" I asked.

"No, no. You go first. Did you return to the scene, as I suggested?"

"Against the orders of the police," interjected Emily.

I grimaced. "Yes, I returned to the scene. The scene of the crime."

"Careful," said Oscar. "You don't yet have evidence a crime's been committed."

"You're right," said Emily. "In all the confusion during the night of the storm and landslip, whoever was in that car could've tried to escape, and simply driven over the edge where the cliff had fallen away."

I smiled at her. "That would've been hard to do from the passenger seat."

"Oh, yes. Perhaps the car rolled over, then?"

"Exactly." Oscar rubbed his chin. "Although, I have information which may make you conclude otherwise."

"Ooh, do tell." Emily grabbed his forearm. "What have you found out from your secret source?"

"All in good time." Oscar broke his scone in half. "Let Shiraz finish first."

I cleared my throat. "When I arrived at the clifftop, the police recovery team were busy. First, they brought up the skeleton in a body bag. Then, with a crane, they lifted the car, dropped it onto a flatbed truck and covered it over. I managed to take a picture before it disappeared under the tarpaulin. Here." I unlocked my phone, found the photo I'd taken and faced it towards him.

Oscar peered over his glasses. "Can you make it bigger?"

"Yes, but if it's the number plate you're wanting, it's J-O-Y 42."

"Joy for two," said Emily. "I'd love a funny number plate for my car."

"No joy for the poor person inside," said Oscar. "But it's great you have the registration. Did you see anything else?"

"Not there, but afterwards, I visited the museum. Among the displays, there was a feature about the great storm and destruction of Golden Beach, with photos of the aftermath and the rescue."

"What a night," said Oscar. "I never want to relive that."

"There was one photo which intrigued me. It was a picture of two people on their wedding day, taken in what looked like a street in a mining or factory town, maybe in the North. And the strange thing was, in the photo's background, decked out with balloons and sprayed with the message 'Just Married', there was a Triumph Spitfire exactly like the one we found at Golden Beach."

"I had a memory of that photo when you mentioned the car originally. That's why I said I had an inkling whose body it was. Did the car have the same number plate?"

"The picture was too grainy to discern it. But the article said the couple were Patrick and Mary Hebblethwaite, and they were unaccounted for after the storm. It didn't say whether they'd ever been found."

Oscar placed down his cup of tea and rubbed his hands together. "We do have a mystery on our hands. And something I've discovered adds to it."

Emily and I both leant towards him, and our heads almost banged.

"Spill the beans, Oscar," I said.

"I, um, may have some information from the pathologist, an old friend of mine." He paused and smiled conspiratorially. "He hasn't released his report yet, but he did tell me the body in the car was a female, probably aged around twenty."

"And?" said Emily. "You've discovered something else, haven't you?"

"Here's the real mystery." Oscar pursed his lips. "Although she had a broken neck, which probably happened when the car rolled over the cliff, that wasn't the only possible cause of death. The pathologist suspects whoever was in the passenger seat may have ingested some kind of poisonous substance."

CHAPTER ELEVEN

Patrick Hebblethwaite sat alone.

He stared at the sky, but it refused to provide him with answers.

He'd spent an entire life ducking and diving, wheeling and dealing, living on the edge of the law, like an unscrupulous antiques dealer.

He'd conducted business with many of their type. The outward front of respectability; the smart jacket, the bow tie, someone the public could trust. The reality: their shop stocked items which walked a fine line between valuable family heirlooms and goods obtained by less-than-respectable means.

He'd always spent his life one step ahead of his detractors.

Always outwitting them.

The police.

His competitors.

The ones who believed he owed them money or favours.

And now?

Now he wasn't sure what his next move would be.

What he should do.

Versus what he was almost definitely going to have to do.

Because the situation he found himself in wasn't one he'd encountered before.

He wasn't uncomfortable with it; far from it. Discomfort with his plight wasn't an emotion familiar to him.

But for the first time, he couldn't see his next move.

So he sat.

And he stared upward.

As if the sky could provide the solution.

CHAPTER TWELVE

"Poison?" asked Emily, raising her eyebrows. "They were murdered?"

Cadbury rolled over at Oscar's feet, let out a sigh and returned to his slumbers. His lips whiffled, and his paws galloped as he dreamt of something more exciting to dogs than a trivial skeleton in a car.

Oscar tilted his head left and right. "Let's not jump to that conclusion. In the chaos that night, they could've accidentally overdosed on prescription medicine."

"Is that likely?" I asked.

"Who knows? The pathologist's sent samples of hair and bone marrow to his colleagues in toxicology. He said it's rare for poison to be present in a body after almost fifty years, but not impossible. We'll have to wait for the toxicologist's report."

"How long will that take?"

"A few days; maybe a week. In the meantime, we should try to find out whether the car in the museum wedding photo was definitely the one in the landslip."

"I've already started that task. The photo said it was copyright of the *Redcliff and Golden Beach Herald*."

"There's a publication I'd forgotten about. I used to read it every day over breakfast."

"The newsagent informed me they store the archives on microfilm at the library, so I visited and filled in a form requesting access to the records from the time of the disaster."

"Gosh. You have been busy."

"Yes," said Emily, grabbing the last scone. "I almost got a parking ticket as she was busy chatting up some chap she met."

"Ah, yes," I said. "A man overheard me asking for the paper's records and introduced himself. He said he used to be the *Herald*'s reporter. Bill Leonard was his name."

"Bill Leonard." Oscar puffed and sat back. "Bill 'the dog' Leonard. He's still alive. I haven't seen him in decades, thank goodness."

"He is still alive. Although, he told me he lives a solitary life. He said he hadn't spoken to anyone for a week before he saw me." I glanced sideways at Oscar. "It doesn't sound like you liked him. Why d'you call him 'the dog'?"

"I knew him as 'the dog' because, when he had hold of what he thought was a good story, no matter how ridiculous, he wouldn't let go. He was like a dog with a rag. An absolute pain in the backside, that chap. The number of times I threw him out of the police station and told him to stop wasting my time. I remember once, he wanted to know why the police weren't investigating kids knocking on people's doors and running away. Remember, in those days, I was the only policeman in town, and I couldn't spend time searching for children playing harmless pranks. He kept badgering me and, in the end, a sensationalist article appeared, intimating I wasn't responding to residents' complaints about a crime spree. I'm not surprised you say he's lonely. He would've run out of people who wanted to speak with him years ago." Oscar paused and sipped his tea. "Bill Leonard. Who would've thought?"

"I'm returning to see him on Thursday," I said. "He mentioned something mysterious. He'd written a story about the aftermath of the Golden Beach landslip, but the editor of the *Herald* at the time refused to publish it, as there wasn't enough evidence."

"Good," said Oscar. "Probably some stupid story about how the landslip was caused by fossil hunters burrowing in the cliff."

"He said the Golden Beach landslip was the only one with a secret. I'll buy him a coffee and see what he has to say when I return to look at the microfilms."

"It can't do any harm, I suppose. He might have an original of that photo you saw at the museum. The chances are, he was the one who took it."

The young, male librarian smiled at me without a hint of recognition. "Yes? Can I help you?"

"I came in on Tuesday and filled in your form to see microfilms of the *Redcliff and Golden Beach Herald* archives."

"Right. Which form was that?"

"Um, D11, I think?"

He called another library employee behind him. "Karen, this woman says she filled in a form D11 on Tuesday. Have we received a completed one?"

I clenched my teeth. "I handed it directly to you."

Karen waddled towards me, holding the form. "Hello. You were requesting to see"—she pushed her glasses up her nose—"the *Redcliff and Golden Beach Herald* archives from February 1976?"

"That's right."

"I'm sorry, Madam. We don't have them."

"Oh. I thought you had all the archives of that paper."

"We do. Just not that particular month. It's most unusual. Every other month is present, apart from February 1976. I checked myself, when processing your request."

"Now what do I do? Is there anywhere else I could search?"

"Um, the Internet?" said the male librarian.

"Great." I shook my head. "You've been very helpful."

Bill Leonard sat at a communal table in the corner of the library, hunched over the previous day's copy of the *Headland Bay Times*. I approached and stood beside him.

He looked up. "Oh. It's you. D'you see this?" He flapped the paper open and jabbed his finger at a photo.

I leant over him. The picture was one that Roy Bartlett had taken while I was standing alongside him, though thankfully I was out of shot. It showed the upside down Triumph Spitfire dangling from the crane, about to be deposited on the flatbed truck. Smaller photos depicted the body bag being recovered and a wide-angle view of the scene.

"Roy Bartlett's article," said Bill. "Only forty-seven years too late." He ran his finger down the text accompanying the images. "This could've all been cleared up in 1976 if they'd only listened to me. Now the land's given up its secrets. And people will finally realise what happened to that person in the body bag."

I crouched down to his level. "Bill, I said I'd buy you a coffee. Come with me and tell me about it."

"It's about time someone listened." Bill pointed at the newspaper again. "They will after this, won't they? They'll see I was right all along." He stood, collected his walking stick and picked up his grocery bag.

"Table for two, please. For hot drinks and cakes."

The staff member at the Bay Hotel showed us to seats which offered a panoramic view of the ocean, glistening in the afternoon sun.

We gazed at the vista, and Bill pointed to a promontory visible to our left. "At the end of the headland, d'you see the lighthouse? That's where the Coastguard base is."

"It must be the one I talk to on the radio. Coastguard Headland Bay." I had a brief thought of Adam, the rope technician, and wondered if he was on duty.

"Are you with Marine Rescue?" asked Mr Leonard. "I knew a man in Redcliff Marine Rescue, back in the '80s. Oscar was his name. He was the Redcliff-upon-Sea policeman as well. Hard work, that chap. Never gave me any tidbits, or an interview. He wouldn't even listen when I provided valuable information about local criminals."

I smiled. "I know Oscar. He runs the Marine Rescue gift shop in his retirement."

"He must be around seventy now. Ten years younger than me. Never could catch up." He laughed. "Give him my regards. I haven't seen him in decades. Stories would've been easier to cover if he'd been more cooperative."

I ordered a double shot skinny latte for me, a regular coffee for Bill and two rounds of cakes.

"Bill, tell me about when you covered the story of the Valentine's Day landslip."

He sighed. "What a day that was. I'm a heavy sleeper, and I slept through the worst of the storm. I woke up to the devastation in Redcliff, the damage to the houses, and the actions of the emergency services. So many brave acts that night went uncatalogued. Your friend Oscar single handedly saved the life of a child trapped when a tree fell through her bedroom. He climbed up the trunk and lifted her through the wreckage to safety."

"Gosh," I said. "He never told me about that."

Bill Leonard wagged a finger at me. "That was one of many similar rescues. The fire brigade carried people to safety from flooded houses. Even your marine rescue volunteers were busy helping pump out inundated buildings. The electricity had failed, so the local farmers banded together and rounded up as many generators as they could to light up the scenes of devastation."

"Did you capture all that on camera?" I asked.

"I was late to the party, but have you seen the records of the newspaper from that time?"

"No. The library couldn't find the microfilms."

"Not to worry. I've kept some black-and-white prints in my private collection, including pictures the paper never published. Anyway, back to that fateful night. I'd heard on the grapevine about the massive cliff collapse at Golden Beach. Reporters from the national newspapers were arriving in town and photographing the devastation in Redcliff, but I reckoned there was a bigger story going on three miles up the road which none of them had cottoned on to. I hitched a ride with a chap who'd come back to Redcliff to fetch a ladder. When I arrived at Golden Beach, I knew I'd nailed the scoop of the decade. Total devastation greeted me. While those national reporters were busy in Redcliff snapping pictures of trees fallen on cars and interviewing people about their missing pets, I was documenting the annihilation of the entire Golden Beach settlement. Houses destroyed. People gathered around bonfires like war refugees. And so many acts of heroism."

The server set down a cup of coffee each and a selection of cakes on a plate. I cast my eyes over the uniformly square offerings and concluded these had definitely not been home made. The not-quite-chocolate taste confirmed this, and I compared them unfavourably to Emily's leftovers. Bill had clearly never visited the Wicked Whelk, as he demolished a vanilla rectangle in one bite.

"But then," he continued, "I sniffed out another drama. One of those little human stories on the edge of a disaster. A tale which would tug at people's emotions and make my writing impossible to put down. Several people died that night at Golden Beach. Many more would have, were it not for the men and women who'd come from Redcliff. Amid the chaos, a local man who was a good organiser began to write a list and account for the residents. Nicholas Murphy was his name. I can still see his face when I think about him."

"I reckon that must be the current Coxswain's father. Murph, we call him. He told me his dad led the rescue convoy from Redcliff to help Golden Beach."

"It has to be the same chap. This Mr Murphy walked among the survivors gathered around the fire or being tended to by people who'd brought bandages and other supplies. He noted their details and also asked for their neighbours' names. In that fashion, he assembled a complete list of all the residents of Golden Beach directly before the storm. He drew a crude aerial layout of the houses as they'd been laid out, and he put a tick beside their inhabitants' names if they'd been found alive, or a cross if it was known they'd passed away. He accounted for everybody except a young couple nobody knew well. They'd not lived there long, and they were renting one of the houses that was destroyed. Everyone presumed they'd been buried in the landslip."

He sipped his coffee, and I watched in his eyes the passion which came from recollecting the events of forty-seven years previously.

"What made you think there was more to it, Bill?"

"A chance remark. A reporter's dream. I sat on the ground, talking with a family huddled around the fire. They had two children: a girl and a boy. And the boy, who was around eight years old, was mad keen on cars, as so many boys of that age are. His mother proudly told me he could look at any car and rattle off the make and model, even the year of manufacture and some features it boasted. And that boy; I don't remember his name, told me his next-door neighbour's car was missing. It transpired this couple who'd disappeared, presumed buried, always parked their sports car in the same spot on the main road, opposite their house." He leant towards me. "The section of asphalt where they parked their car had survived the disaster. But it was empty. And I quickly realised that if the car was missing, it was unlikely the young couple were buried in the landslip. The chances of them both perishing in the cliff collapse, and their car being stolen by persons unknown in the same event was a stretch of imagination too far. Either they'd left the area before the storm, or…"

I sucked in a breath. "Did you ask the boy to tell you the make and model?"

"I did."

"Was it a blue Triumph Spitfire?"

"Indeed. A blue, 1974, Mark IV Spitfire. And I'm willing to bet the same car's turned up in Roy Bartlett's photo."

CHAPTER THIRTEEN

I grimaced as I sipped my cold coffee. The weather had turned, and the wind whipped whitecaps across the dark-grey sea. Along the path to the lighthouse, low bushes bowed in the breeze, and I watched a dog walker wrap her coat tightly around herself and bend her body into the gale.

"What did you do next, Bill?"

"I returned to the newspaper office, typed up my report about the missing couple and gave the lab my film to be developed. I told the editor to hold tomorrow's front page."

"And did he?"

"Far from it." Bill pinched his lips together, stared into his lap and shook his head. "He'd already compiled a story about the devastation in Redcliff and bought photos from an agency photographer. Can you believe he yelled at me because I'd slept through the storm? He told me I should've been up all night, snapping the action in Redcliff, where most of our readers lived. He told me I'd failed. A massive news event, and I'd missed it."

"Surely you could persuade him. You had the photos from Golden Beach."

"I pleaded with the editor. I told him I thought there was another story, a bigger story, but it would take some investigation. He didn't object to printing my photos of the cliff collapse, but as for my mystery of the missing couple; he dismissed it. He was convinced the young people in question, who nobody knew anyway, weren't even in Golden Beach during the storm. They'd come from away; maybe they'd gone back home before the storm struck? I clearly remember his words: 'Bill, you've got no story at all. What's the headline? A couple might've perished in the storm, but we don't know. Stop wasting my time'."

"Did you investigate further?"

"The editor wouldn't allow me to work on it. He needed me to 'redeem myself'; to get busy in Redcliff, speak with those who'd lost everything, interview the rescuers, photograph the clean-up operation." Bill wagged a finger at me. "Don't forget, this was the biggest storm the area had suffered in almost two hundred years."

"I know. I saw the exhibits in the museum."

"As soon as the excitement died down, and other more mundane items had taken over the front pages, I asked the editor for a week off. I told him covering the event had exhausted me. This wasn't true; I had more energy than ever. I honestly thought exposing this mystery would rocket my career into the big time: a book deal, movie options, maybe a job at one of the big Fleet Street papers."

"What did you do first?"

"I needed to find out who the young couple were. No one knew their surname, or where they'd come from. So I made discreet inquiries around Redcliff, whilst being careful not to draw attention to my end game. I didn't want word of my investigation to get back to my editor. Then I had a stroke of luck. I told the chap at the local car repair garage a white lie. I said I was thinking of buying a Triumph Spitfire and wondered if he knew of any for sale. He said he didn't, but mentioned a customer had brought him a Spitfire for an oil change recently, and he suggested I ask him if he wanted to sell it. Of course, when I heard this, I tried not to look too eager, but I couldn't wait to discover the details. The garage man dug through his filing cabinet, found the invoice for the servicing, and there was the name and address at the top. Patrick Hebblethwaite, 8, Headland Bay Road, Golden Beach."

"An unusual name," I said. "I saw it in the museum display. There can't be too many people with the surname Hebblethwaite."

Bill shook his head. "No indeed. And you're right, Patrick Hebblethwaite was the name of the man in the paper. But we're jumping ahead."

We were the last clients in the tea and coffee area, and hotel staff had begun preparing for the evening dinner service around us.

"After you discovered this man's name, what next?"

Bill picked up the last cake, a brown cube with red jelly wobbling on top, and placed it on his plate. "As you noted, Hebblethwaite's an uncommon surname. I called a contact of mine, a genealogist. I invented a story about wanting to trace someone with the surname Hebblethwaite for a newspaper article, which wasn't strictly untrue, was it? He told me the name originates from a specific area in the North of England, a cluster of villages in a rural farming area. Apparently, it means 'a clearing by a wooden bridge' in the local dialect." Bill lowered his voice. "Three days remained of my leave of absence. I took the night train. My destination: the nearest station to the cluster of villages. The journey took me twelve hours including two changes of train during the night. I was like a bloodhound on a scent; I couldn't let this go."

I recalled Oscar's nickname for Bill: 'The dog'.

He continued. "Once I'd arrived at my final destination, a tiny, country railway station called Hebble Bridge, I had another stroke of luck. In the station ticket hall, I discovered a business card pinned to a corkboard. *Frank Hebblethwaite: Taxi Driver. Call me for your transport needs.* I knew I'd arrived at the right place."

"Gosh. That was lucky. So you rang him?"

"Indeed, I did. From the station payphone. Not least because I'd no idea where I was going. He turned up after a few minutes in a large saloon, and I asked him to drive me to Patrick Hebblethwaite's house. During the journey, I inquired if they were related. He explained they were third or maybe fourth cousins; he didn't know Patrick well. I mentioned I didn't know him either, but I had a message for him from a neighbour. Again, not strictly a lie."

I laughed and tossed my hair back at Bill's reporter cunning. "The truth's becoming more bent than a broken boomerang. Where did he take you?"

"We drove through winding country lanes, narrower than the ones around here. He asked me where I'd come from, and I answered in very general terms. I'm sure he was becoming more suspicious as the journey progressed, but he could hardly refuse to take his fare to the destination requested, could he? After around twenty minutes' drive, we arrived at a remote, detached stone cottage standing alone in the lee of a range of hills. I paid him, and he asked me if I wanted him to wait. I declined his offer, and he drove away."

I shifted in my seat. Bill's story was gripping, and I needed to know how it ended, but my bottom had gone to sleep.

"A light was on downstairs," continued Bill, "so I knew someone was in. Once Frank's car had departed, I banged on the door and waited. I remember it was a blue door, rotted around the edges. Faint footsteps sounded from the other side, and my heart pounded as I wondered whether the man who'd lived at 8, Headland Bay Road, Golden Beach, would open it. But the door was unlatched by an elderly woman."

"Who was she?" I asked. Ours was now the last table in the hotel that the staff hadn't laid with white linen tablecloths for dinner, but there was no way I'd vacate my seat before Bill finished his story.

"She greeted me with the words, 'Yes, sir?' in the deferential way country folk address a stranger, and I told her my name, and that I was looking for Patrick Hebblethwaite. She ushered me into a dim, stone-floored kitchen, where a fire burnt in a hearth, causing me to wonder if this remote farmhouse even had electricity. The room centred around a solid, rectangular, wooden table, and seated at it was an old man. I presumed he was the woman's husband. 'Patrick,' she shouted at him, as you might to someone who's very deaf. 'There's a Mr Leonard to see you.'"

Bill paused.

"Exactly how old was this man?" I asked.

He scratched his head, and I could see his mind reliving the scene forty-seven years previously. "I reckon he was around seventy, but he had the rough, weathered look of those who work the land, and he could've been ten years younger. He'd clearly had a physical life."

"But he wasn't the man from Golden Beach?"

"He couldn't have been. Those people were described as a young couple. I know the word 'young' can be subjective, especially now in the 2020s, but these farmers were anything but youthful. I asked him if he was Patrick Hebblethwaite, and he replied he was, which left me in a conundrum. So I inquired if there was anyone else called Patrick Hebblethwaite; perhaps the taxi driver had taken me to the wrong house. 'Not around here,' the old man said. 'Not anymore.' I asked him what he meant by 'not anymore.' The elderly couple glanced at each other, and the wife spoke. She told me their son was called Patrick, named after his father."

"Gosh," I said. "He must've been the Golden Beach chap. Did they say where you would find him?"

Bill shook his head. "The old man said they hadn't seen him in weeks, and they never would again. He told me he wouldn't even speak his name. He said as far as they were concerned, he was dead."

"That's dramatic," I said. "Did he mean he'd died in the landslip?"

"No, this couple didn't know anything about the landslip." Bill wiped his mouth with a serviette and continued. "The old lady wagged her finger at her husband. 'You mustn't speak like that,' she said. 'He's still our son.' And then the old man turned to me. 'I have no son,' he said. 'And who are you to be asking?' I told him I had a message for him. 'You won't find him here,' said Patrick Hebblethwaite, senior. 'Good day to you.' And with that, he turned his back to me and refused to engage in any more conversation."

Bill exhaled hard. I considered buying him another cup of coffee, but I wasn't sure the wait staff would serve me anything but a full meal this late in the afternoon.

"So you'd had a wasted journey?" I asked.

Bill's mind returned to that dark farmer's cottage in the hills. "The old woman showed me out of the kitchen, back to the front door. 'I'm sorry, sir,' she said. 'He hasn't been himself since Patrick disappeared.' I asked her when that was, and what precipitated this reaction from her husband. She related the tale of their son's departure, as we stood inside the front porch, out of the old man's earshot."

I clasped my hands and leant forwards towards Bill.

"Apparently," he continued, "the younger Patrick Hebblethwaite had taken up with a girl. Mary, her name was. They'd met in the local town and begun courting. One day, not much later, Patrick announced to his parents he was going to ask Mary to be his wife. The old woman said they were both pleased for him, as they'd always worried he'd end up as a bachelor, living by himself in a draughty old farmhouse. Her husband asked him to bring Mary around to meet them. The old lady said she'd spent the day baking, and she'd laid out the tablecloth and best china in the front parlour; a room they never used unless they had important guests, such as the village priest. I recall she paused and made the sign of the cross at this point, and I didn't push her for more details. That's an old journalist's trick; don't fill someone's silence."

"And after she'd crossed herself…?" I prompted.

"This is the good bit," said Bill, grinning and rubbing his hands together. "What I think is the crux of the whole mystery. Mary arrived, and they were pleased to see she was a sweet young girl, nothing too fast about her, nothing too fancy. Mary was ill at ease, she recalled, but they put that down to nervousness about meeting them for the first time. They served tea in the parlour, and she complimented the baking, and showed an interest in the farm, and they could see their boy's pleasure that they seemed to approve of his choice of wife. The conversation moved on to the forthcoming wedding, and where they wanted to hold it. In those days, tradition dictated a wedding was always held at the bride's church. Patrick Hebblethwaite, the father, asked Mary which church she attended. And her reply was that she worshipped at Saint Michael's."

Bill looked up at me. "Don't forget, I was a complete stranger to these parts. These country folk hardly ever left the few villages which made up their local area. This old woman believed she'd told me the complete story, and nothing needed further explanation."

"So you asked her to clarify?"

"I did," said Bill. "I asked her, what was wrong with Saint Michael's? And she shook her head and told me at that point they realised Mary was a Protestant. I said, I didn't understand. Then she dropped the bombshell. 'We're Catholics, my husband and I,' she said. 'And our son. We christened him at the Church of the Holy Assumption. When he told us his intended wife's name was Mary, we assumed she was Catholic too. The chances of my husband letting his son marry a Protestant… hell would freeze over before that happened. I'm more understanding; I didn't mind, so long as our son was happy, but my husband was upset he'd even allowed her in the house. He stood, pointed at the door with an outstretched arm and said they'd be getting married over his dead body. And our son faced up to him, told his father he was marrying Mary regardless, and said if his father didn't approve, they'd elope.' I asked the old lady if that was what had happened. Then she reached into a shopping bag hanging on a coat hook behind the front door, extracted a dog-eared piece of paper and handed it to me. It was a black-and-white photo; a newspaper cutting."

"What did it say?" I asked. I could hardly breathe, listening to the conclusion of Bill's story.

"She told me her friend had sent it to her, and she didn't dare show it to Patrick senior. She said neither of them had seen their son since that day, and they didn't know where he was. The photo showed a young couple dressed in what would've passed for their smartest clothes, standing in front of a car decorated for a wedding. I told her I didn't know where her son was either, but I knew where he'd been living recently, and I was trying to track both him and Mary down. I asked her if I could copy the photo. She laid it on their hall table, and I photographed it with the instant camera I always carried with me. And that's the picture, Shiraz, in the newspaper article you saw in the museum."

CHAPTER FOURTEEN

A staff member approached us. "Excuse me? We need this table for dinner service. You're welcome to continue your conversation in the public bar."

"Oh, sorry." I looked at my phone. "Gosh, is that the time? It's okay; we'll leave now."

I held the door to the street open for Bill.

"What did you think of that story?" he asked. "D'you understand my frustration at not being allowed to investigate further?"

"It's fascinating," I said. "But it asks more questions than it answers."

"Exactly, young lady, exactly."

Light rain fell, and the pavement glistened in the hotel's lights.

"Would you like to walk back to my house?" he asked. "I could show you my photos. The ones which have never been published." He jabbed his walking stick toward the back streets, away from the sea.

"I'd love to. But the evening bus to Redcliff-upon-Sea leaves soon. If I miss it, I'll be stuck in Headland Bay. Could I return and see them next week?"

"Any time," said Bill. "You know where to find me. Same place, every afternoon, in the library reading the papers. I've enjoyed our chat; I don't think I've had such a long conversation in years."

I shook his hand. "Bill, I intend to get to the bottom of this historical mystery."

"I hope you do," he said, as the bus pulled up, and the doors opened. "I hope you succeed where I didn't."

We sat at Oscar's dining room table that evening sharing a bottle of Merlot. Oscar gazed into his wine glass while Emily and I waited for him to digest my retelling of Bill's story.

"This is a riddle, isn't it?" he said. "There were many loose ends from that night and, I dare say, many loops went unclosed."

"Do you think this is a murder case?" asked Emily. "Because if it is, could we please call the police and let them deal with it? I don't want anything scary to happen again."

"They're already dealing with it, in a manner of speaking," said Oscar. "Although how many resources they'll assign investigating such a cold case is anyone's guess."

I grinned and leant forward. "Let's pretend it was murder. I mean, it could be, right? Just for fun, let's recap those events of forty-seven years ago, and see if we can deduce who might've killed the poor girl in the car, and why."

"You have a strange idea of fun," said Emily. "Could we play a board game instead?"

Oscar rubbed his hands together. "Solving a murder is in many ways like a board game. Chess, for instance. Constantly trying to outwit your opponent, work out what their next move is, or even their next ten moves."

"There is a board game based on a murder hunt, isn't there?" I said. "Cluedo. Let's play real-life Cluedo."

"Okay," said Emily. "The murderer was Patrick Hebblethwaite, with the poison, in the car, on the landslip. I win." She raised both arms in a victory stance. "Case closed."

"Not so fast," I said. "We have other suspects too. How about Patrick Hebblethwaite senior? According to Bill, he didn't approve of his son's choice of wife because of his religious beliefs, and he refused to speak to his son ever again if they married. Maybe he discovered they'd tied the knot, and he murdered Mary, or arranged for her to be murdered, in a bid to see his son again?"

"He could've simply accepted their marriage," said Emily.

"I feel he was too proud for that. Too stubborn."

"And there's a third suspicious party," said Oscar, "although, at the moment, I can only see the most tenuous connection between them and the deceased."

"Who?" Emily and I asked simultaneously.

"The scruffy man with the dog."

"Really?" I said. "I'd forgotten about him. Why d'you think he could be the murderer?"

"As I said, it's a tenuous connection. But he's the right age, although rough sleepers often look older than their years. You found him on the beach when it was closed, and earlier the same day, he'd been in the gift shop asking me about the night of the landslip. Plus, you mentioned he had an accent from away. Not a local man. Let's not rule him out. He was acting suspiciously. And Cadbury didn't like his dog. He has a good nose for suspicious personalities, don't you, boy?" Oscar addressed this to the chocolate Labrador, who cocked his head to one side, pricked up his ears, then returned to a half sleep with one eye open, in case we required him for further psychological profiling.

"That's three suspects," I said. "Is there anyone else we know who was present at the event, and could've done the deed?"

"The newspaper reporter chap?" said Emily.

"Bill Leonard?" Oscar shook his head. "Most unlikely. He was a pain in the backside, but no murderer. Begrudgingly, I'll admit he was good at his job, and a well-known member of the press. I won't say well-respected. Reporters are like estate agents. You only talk to them when you have to."

"And he wasn't there on the night," I said. "He turned up the following day to interview people and take photos."

"That's all then," said Emily. "Because any suspects in this case, by definition, need to be over sixty years old. So that narrows it down."

"Or dead," said Oscar.

"Or dead," I echoed. "Actually, that's a good way to rule people out. We should be able to discover fairly easily if someone's alive or dead."

Oscar wagged one finger. "You're forgetting something fundamental."

"What?"

"Just because someone's dead doesn't mean they're innocent."

"That'd be a waste of time," said Emily. "If we spent ages investigating, and then we discovered the murderer was dead themselves." She yawned loudly, which startled Cadbury. He jumped up and shook himself.

"We must be going," I said. "But this is intriguing. A historical mystery."

"Yep, we need to get to bed," said Emily. "Marine rescue training on the boat tomorrow afternoon."

"Gosh, is it Saturday tomorrow? I wonder what Murph will pull out of his surprise box of tricks. Bye, Oscar. Thanks for the wine."

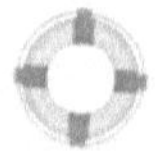

The sound of Emily tugging on clothes, running down the stairs and slamming the door to the street woke me. I didn't envy her opening the café at 6:00 a.m., but there was no way I'd accompany her; this time was far too early for me. I made a silent promise to help her clear up later, pulled the duvet over my shoulders and returned to sleep. At 9:30, my phone pinged twice, so I stuffed it under a pillow and turned over. On the third ping, I opened my eyes fully and wondered if three pings in two minutes deserved my attention. Boots was stretched out across the pillow and swiped a claw violently when I relocated him to find the device.

> Crew

That was the first ping. One word.

> For today's training

Okay, it came from Murph. Not the most technically capable man ever.

> Remember to bring your workbooks

Was that it? Remember to bring your workbooks?

A fourth ping.

> And revise the section on fire

Oh, great. Was Murph going to make me recall all the different fire classes again and the various types of fire extinguisher? I pulled back the covers, hopped up to look in the mirror and decided I needed a double shot skinny latte, a hot shower and a hair-detangle before my workbook received my attention.

The rescue vessel powered away from Redcliff Harbour. Emily and I held on tight and shared a grin as cool salt spray drenched our waterproofs. This was real living. Training to save lives and make a difference. Nothing like my old, vapid, it-girl existence. I wondered if we'd encounter Adam, the Coastguard rope technician, again. My mind drifted off thinking about him. Maybe forty years old, strong, rugged, and capable. Although, he hadn't shown any interest in me. That was the old me, imagining every man found me irresistible. New Shiraz was a real person who didn't need expensive clothes and makeup to impress.

I hoped.

Murph brought the boat to a stop almost out of sight of land, and the coast appeared off the starboard side as a thin, dark strip on the horizon. I welcomed its presence, though I knew if anything bad happened, we had no chance of swimming that far.

"Right, crew," he said. "We're a long way from shore, and one of the boat's engines catches fire. What do we do?"

"Douse the fire blanket in sea water and cover the engine in question," I replied.

"Very good, Shiraz. You've brushed up since your last effort."

Phew. My no-study method of learning's working well.

"Anything else?" asked Murph.

"Um, call for help?"

"Definitely," said Murph. "Call for help. What information should we give in the call?"

Emily put her hand up.

"No need to raise your hand." said Murph. "This isn't kindergarten."

"Our position, the number of people on board and the nature of the problem."

"Very good. Anything else?" He looked at me.

"Um, the size of our boat?" I said, "So anyone coming to help knows what they're dealing with."

"We could do, I suppose. There's something more important than that."

Emily and I glanced at each other. I shrugged.

"David?" asked Murph.

"Our boat registration and call sign," said David. "Ours is Redcliff Marine Rescue. Anyone calling back, or coming to our aid, needs to know who they're looking for."

"Wouldn't they search for the only burning boat?"

Murph pointed. "Look back at the land, Shiraz. What d'you see?"

"A dark-grey strip above the water."

"D'you reckon you could tell where a fire was burning on the land from this distance?"

"Not unless it was a massive one, like a factory blaze."

"Exactly. So how would a rescue vessel coming from the shore be able to see our little boat puffing smoke from its engine? We need to tell them as much information as we can."

The radio burst into life. "Marine Rescue Redcliff, this is Coastguard Headland Bay. Come in, please. Over."

David snatched the transmitter from its cradle. "Coastguard Headland Bay, this is Marine Rescue Redcliff. Receiving. Over."

"Please proceed to Golden Beach. A member of the public's reported a fire burning on the shingle. We understand there's no immediate danger to life, but please check it out. Over."

"Received. Proceeding to Golden Beach to check a fire burning on shore. Over."

"What is your ETA? Over."

David peered at the instruments. "ETA fifteen minutes. Over."

"We'll dispatch a shore crew to assist. Please advise when you're on scene. Over."

"Confirming we'll advise you when we're at Golden Beach. Over."

"Coastguard Headland Bay out."

"That's a coincidence," said Murph, taking the helm. "We were talking about fire, and now we have one. Everybody hold on."

"Holding on," we all responded, as Murph powered up the engines and headed towards the shoreline. I admired how he knew exactly which direction to go without so much as a glance at the navigation instruments.

"Why would there be a fire on the beach?" I shouted at the back of Murph's head.

"Good question," he yelled over the sound of the motors. "In summer, we're often called to reports of fires which turn out to be teenagers having a beach party, cooking some sausages, sharing some underage beers, harmless stuff. It's unusual in March."

"Remember that job with the fire at Smuggler's Cove, near the vicarage?" asked David.

"The one where a glass bottle set the scrub at the back of the beach alight?" said Murph. "Biggest fire I've ever seen."

"Glass bottle?" asked Emily. "Did it act like a magnifying glass?"

"Yep," said David. "The sun shone through the discarded bottle and reflected intense heat onto the dry bushes. You've heard the expression 'tinder-dry'? That's what it refers to."

The rescue boat bounced across the waves and rounded a promontory.

"Did you put the fire out?" I asked.

"What, with our little fire extinguisher?" Murph laughed. "The Coastguard helicopter picked up its bucket attachment, scooped up masses of seawater and dumped it on the blaze. Very exciting; like the wildfires overseas on the news. There's nothing like that here normally."

"So we don't fight fires with our gear?"

"We could, if it was a tiny one," said David. "But only if you've completed fire training. If we elect to tackle this fire at Golden Beach, only Murph and I are qualified to do it."

I get it, David; you're more experienced than me.

My thoughts drifted to when, or whether, I'd see Adam again.

I didn't have long to wait. Golden Beach came into view and, on the shore, a small pile of wood and rubbish smouldered. A tall man and woman, both in Coastguard overalls, stood next to it, addressing a stooped, smaller figure with a thin coat draped around him.

His short, stumpy dog barked at us, and I realised exactly who we were looking at.

CHAPTER FIFTEEN

"It's that scruffy man and his dog again," I called out to my colleagues, as Murph slowed the boat down.

"Shimmering stern lights," he exclaimed. "The chap we escorted from Golden Beach last week? What's he doing back here?"

The Coastguard figures turned towards the sea as our boat chugged into the shallows, and my heart beat a little faster as I identified the taller one as Adam.

Murph anchored the vessel within wading distance, while David flicked a catch on the fire extinguisher bracket and lifted the appliance free. "Shiraz, could you jump in with me? Looks like the dog wants to be friends again." He laughed and leapt into the shallow water, holding the extinguisher over his head.

Oh, great. Rebel the runner.

I turned around and flipped myself over the side after him.

David aimed our fire extinguisher at the smoking pile of dead wood and pulled the trigger, sweeping the foam back and forth until the fire was out.

He nodded at the Coastguard team, then addressed the scruffy man. "Are you hurt at all, sir? What are you doing here again? We reminded you to stay away from Golden Beach because of the landslip."

"I'm sorry, Officer," the man gibbered. "I'm not hurt, just cold." He attempted to stifle his cough.

Rebel sniffed my waterproofs, then sat and looked up at me as if I'd secreted a fillet steak in my pocket. I glanced at his owner and wondered why he still wore sunglasses on this dark, stormy day.

Adam spoke to David. "We received a call about the fire on the beach and found this gentleman sitting next to it, keeping himself warm." He lowered his voice. "He seems to be of no fixed abode. It's possible he's been living here." He turned to me. "Hello, we've met before, haven't we?"

Several men had tried this pickup line at various nightclubs and parties over the years, but this was the first time it was true. And I didn't want it to be true. The last thing I needed was for David and Murph to discover Emily and I had been rescued from the landslip.

"Hi," I replied, but my voice squeaked and came out like I was a three-year-old. I cleared my throat and deliberately tried to speak lower. "Hi. Have we met? I'm sorry, I've a terrible memory for faces." I quickly turned to David. "What shall we do with the man and the dog this time?"

"We'll have to remove him on our boat again." He swivelled to face Adam. "You won't be able to extract him, will you?"

"It'd be quicker if you take him back to Redcliff with you."

"Okay, that makes sense." David spoke to the scruffy man again. "This'll be the same procedure as before, sir. You put your arm around my neck, and I'll pick you up. Shiraz'll grab your dog."

"Shiraz! That's it," exclaimed Adam. "I know where we met. You and your friend were the ladies we resc…"

At that moment, Rebel realised I didn't have any steaks in my pockets and took off across the beach.

"Sorry!" I shouted over my shoulder as I ran after him. "I have to catch the dog."

Phew. Saved by the mutt.

Rebel led me along the beach, parallel to the breaking waves. He stopped, turned around and faced me, a silly grin on his face, and his tongue lolling to one side. He loved this game. Unfortunately, I didn't. I lunged at him, and he turned tail and ran off again. As we neared the base of the landslip, the dog paused to sniff at some litter, and I managed to seize his collar.

The distraction was a small, glass bottle with an unusual shape, nothing like the soft drinks found in Redcliff's grocery store. It was discoloured and blackened, as if it had been in a fire. I remembered the story David and Murph related about a glass bottle starting a blaze, and I decided to take the bottle with me. Rebel tugged, and I worried my arm would detach from my shoulder with his strength. I was glad I'd exercised regularly throughout my thirties; my ex-husband's insistence on an expensive gym membership to keep my body magazine photo-fit had certainly paid off today. I entered the water carrying the dog and passed him up to the rescue boat, then heaved myself on board.

Emily had wrapped the old man in our fire blanket, and I made a mental note to run it through the washing machine. Preferably the one at the town laundrette, not Emily's. David slipped a cowl over the man's head to keep him warm. He shivered, and I noticed his lips were turning blue, which I knew from first aid training was an early sign of hypothermia.

Murph clanked up the anchor. "Everybody holding on?" he called. "Going up."

Our speed increased, and we bounced across the waves to the marine rescue base. I shielded the scruffy man from the wind, while trying to keep my distance from his odour, which had increased in intensity. He disappeared inside the blanket and coughed so hard I was worried he'd dislocate a rib.

Once we reached Redcliff Harbour, David and I tied the boat up, and Murph carried the man into the marine rescue building.

He called to us. "Shiraz, put the heating on. Boil the kettle. Make a hot, sweet cup of tea. Emily, call for an ambulance. Tell them we have a hypothermic male aged around seventy years old. Then grab as many blankets as you can; anything you can find."

"What are you two doing with him?" I asked, as David finished on the boat and dashed past me to help Murph.

"Putting him in a lukewarm shower," yelled Murph.

I knew the old man smelt bad, but I felt washing him was beyond our lifesaving responsibilities.

"Warming him up," David clarified, and I heard the hiss of running water. Although I'd completed my first aid training, it hadn't mentioned showers. There was no way I'd want to see that vagrant guy naked. I turned the heating control to full, filled the kettle and prepared tea. Emily rang the ambulance, and I overheard parts of her conversation. We both stripped off our waterproofs as the room took on the atmosphere of a Turkish bath.

The hiss of the hot water continued for considerably longer than a normal shower might take. Okay, I admit, I had been known to take the occasional sixty-minute shower when returning from a hard night at a society engagement but, generally, showers are brief affairs.

"Shiraz, could you find more towels?" yelled Murph. "Second locker from the right in the changing room."

"Is everything okay?"

"No. He's still showing signs of hypothermia, and we're trying to increase his body temperature."

"Is he going to die?"

"Not on my watch. Emily, where's the ambulance?"

"Not here yet. Shall I call them again?"

"You did tell them we had an elderly, hypothermic patient, didn't you?"

"Exactly as you instructed."

"Go outside and look out for them."

"Right away." Emily opened the door and as she stepped onto the harbour wall, we heard distant sirens.

"The ambulance is nearly here," I called to everyone. "More towels, Murph." I shoved four blue-and-white bath sheets into the shower room.

The wail of the ambulance sounded outside. I heard Emily's rapid summary of the situation and expected the crew to sprint in rolling a trolley in front of them, grab the patient, bundle him into the back and race off with the blue lights flashing, and the sirens screaming.

None of this happened. Emily led the two crew into our breakout room, and they calmly laid down their medical equipment bags. One was a woman with a ponytail. The other, a movie-star-handsome Indian man with a closely cropped black beard, a red turban and circular spectacles.

"Good afternoon," said the male paramedic. He had an upper-class, educated accent. "I'm Karam, and this is Darcy. Where is the patient, please?"

"In the back. We're trying to keep him warm." I felt the paramedics should be showing more urgency, but then I realised their calm demeanour prevented others from panicking.

"Why is he here?"

I thought this a strange question. "We rescued him from Golden Beach. He was in the open air on this freezing afternoon, and he'd lit a fire to keep warm. I think he may've been sleeping rough."

"How have you treated him so far?"

I felt like saying, 'Better than he deserved,' but I realised this wasn't his meaning. "We wrapped him in our fire blanket, brought him here, and my colleagues are bathing him in a lukewarm shower."

"It's lucky they've kept it lukewarm," said Karam. "A hypothermic patient can suffer from low blood pressure in hot water. Could you show us to the shower room, please?"

I led them to the rear of the marine rescue station, where the ambulance crew greeted Murph and David.

"Thanks for looking after him," said Darcy. "Let's take him out of the shower, wrap him up and give him a warm drink."

I averted my eyes as Murph and David lifted the man from the cubicle. They dried him with towels, wrapped him in blankets and carried him to the breakout room, which now reminded me of the sauna in a luxury resort. I added a thick jumper to his coverings which I'd found in a bin marked 'lost property'. For some reason, he still wore his oversize sunglasses.

He didn't look well.

"Hi, I'm Darcy," said the woman. "I'll look after you. What's your name?"

The man coughed uncontrollably, then looked up at her. "Who are you?"

That accent again. A mixture of London's East End and somewhere in the North.

She spoke more distinctly. "I'm a paramedic. I'm here to care for you."

"Where am I?"

"You're in Redcliff Marine Rescue's building," said Karam. "The crew saved you from the beach. You were very cold. Stay still while I take your temperature." He removed a white, plastic heat scanner from a small bag and beeped it at the man's forehead. "Thirty-four." He turned to Darcy, and in a different, more direct voice said, "Anterior torso heat pad, please."

Darcy removed a flat cushion from a bag and applied it to the man's back, under the thick jumper. The patient stared directly at Karam through his sunglasses and swallowed a cough. "Am I in India?"

Karam laughed; a deep, educated laugh.

"You're not in India," he said. "My parents are Indian, but I was born in London, and I've lived in England all my life." He turned to me and spoke quietly. "Confusion's a common symptom of hypothermia."

I loved the sound of his private-school accent and didn't want him to stop talking.

"Will you take him to the hospital?" asked Emily.

"Yes," said Karam, "but we'll try to raise his temperature before we move him. Is his warm drink ready? Make it milky, please; not too hot."

Emily passed Karam the tea, and he gave it to the man to hold. "Sip this slowly. It may not be how you have your tea usually, but it'll warm you from inside. We'll take your temperature again in a minute. Could you tell us your name?"

The man took a sip of tea, spluttered, turned to me accusingly and said, "Where's Rebel?"

131

CHAPTER SIXTEEN

Rebel. Oh, no. We left the dog on the boat.

"Who's Rebel?" Darcy asked the man. "Was someone else with you?"

"No," I said. "Rebel's his dog. I'll fetch him."

"Good idea," said Darcy. "He could hug the dog, and it'd help with warming him up."

I was about to say I didn't think Rebel was a very huggable dog, when I heard barking outside, accompanied by the unmistakable banshee yowl of a cat in distress.

Emily rushed out, yelled and clapped. "Get away. Get away from him."

She returned with an exceptionally annoyed Boots in her arms, wide eyed, with his fur puffed up like a gigantic orange porcupine, and his tail as broad as a lavatory brush. "That slavering beast cornered Boots. Look at him, poor thing." She stroked the ginger cat, who wriggled and attempted to peek over her shoulder, presumably to see if the slavering beast had followed them inside. "It's okay, Boots," she soothed. "You're safe now. Horrible doggy's gone."

"Um, did you see where the horrible doggy went?" I asked. "We should find him and maybe tie him to something."

"Take a short line from the rope locker," said Murph. "And stick your nose in the fridge. I think there are leftover pizza slices from the committee meeting last night. You could tempt him with one."

"You could tempt me with one, too," said the scruffy man.

Colour was returning to his cheeks, and he looked brighter, although his cough wouldn't go away.

"They'll give you food at the hospital," said Karam. "May I take your temperature again?" He pointed the white thermometer at the man's forehead. "Thirty-five point five. Almost back to normal. D'you feel well enough to ride in the ambulance? You still haven't told us your name, sir."

"I'm not going without Rebel."

"Sorry, sir. I can't take a dog with us, and I'm sure they won't allow it in the hospital. Is there anyone who could look after Rebel for you?"

"Um, we have to find him first," I said.

Karam looked at me, and I met his eyes. "Would you mind retrieving the dog, Ms...?"

"Shiraz," I said. "My name's Shiraz."

"Shiraz. I like that name." He smiled. "Would you mind finding the gentleman's dog and looking after it?"

"Um, yes. Anything to help."

"That mutt's not coming into my flat," said Emily. "What about Boots?" She stroked the cat, whose saucer-sized eyes betrayed his recent experience.

"Don't call Rebel a mutt," objected the patient, who was recovering rather too much for my liking. "He's not a mutt. He's a therapy companion animal."

"He is?" I asked, probably more rudely than I should have. "Let's find him, and we'll work something out." I smiled at Karam, nodded at Darcy as she packed up their equipment and ran out to find the mutt. The therapy companion animal. Whatever.

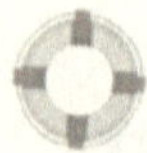

It didn't take me long to track down Rebel. A discarded takeaway chicken box had distracted him, and he'd been licking it so hard his tongue had ripped through the cardboard. I held out a slice of pizza. "Here, Rebel. Remember me? We're old friends. Who wants some yummy food?"

Rebel turned away from the chicken, raised his nose to the air and sniffed. He walked towards me suspiciously and stopped a foot in front of the cheesy triangle of delight. I hoped he wasn't already full of fried chicken.

"Here, boy. Come and get the pizza. Come on." I waggled the slice enticingly as if it were alive.

Rebel shuffled forward an inch.

"Rebel, you know you want it. Here, boy." I held the pizza out further, then glanced over my shoulder as the beeping of the reversing ambulance sounded behind me. As I turned away, Rebel grabbed the triangle out of my fingers and took off.

"Come back, you mutt." I sprinted after him as he ran with the pizza in his mouth.

A young couple walked along the promenade towards me.

"Hey," I yelled. "Can you stop that dog?"

The man tried to rugby tackle Rebel, who jumped over him and continued running. I shouted, "Thanks, and sorry," then we persisted with our ludicrous chase along the seafront. We dodged evening joggers, caused a cyclist to swerve into railings and scared a pensioner who shook her walking stick at us.

"Keep your dog under control," she called.

"He's not my dog," I yelled back as we raced past.

I was glad I'd kept up my fitness regime all those years in London. A five-mile jog across Hampstead Heath was a daily event in those days, but I hadn't persevered since I'd lived in Redcliff, and Rebel showed no sign of relenting. And to cap it all, he'd swallowed the pizza, and now I had no other ammunition to tempt him with.

We were about to reach the far end of the promenade, where the seafront met the bottom of the High Street. Although Rebel wasn't my number one favourite dog, I had to catch him before he reached the road. The last thing I needed was him causing havoc in the main thoroughfare.

As we rounded the last corner, I heard a deeper bark than Rebel's. Rebel screeched to a halt, turned tail and sprinted back towards me, pursued by Oscar's big chocolate Labrador. Rebel now saw me as his saviour and protector and, as he reached me, I scooped him up and held the wriggling canine bundle tightly.

"Quiet, Cadbury," shouted Oscar, appearing around the corner. "Hello, Shiraz. What's this? D'you have a dog?"

"He's not mine," I said, as Rebel squirmed in my arms, and Cadbury sat at my feet and eyed him. "But I appreciate Cadbury helping me catch him."

Oscar pointed. "I know that dog. He belongs to the rough sleeper who came into my shop. What are you doing with him?"

"It's a long story. I promise I'll tell you but, in the meantime, is there any chance you could house him for the night? His owner's been taken to hospital, and somehow I seem to have become his foster parent. There's no way Emily and I can keep a dog at our place. Boots and him already met, and the encounter wasn't a success."

"Yes, he looks like a cat chaser. D'you have a lead for him?"

"No, but I have a length of rope I brought from Marine Rescue in my left coat pocket."

Oscar reached into my pocket while I gripped Rebel with both hands. He tied it expertly around Rebel's collar with a bowline knot, and this action reminded me he'd been a rescue skipper many years ago. I hoped my bowlines looked as good when it came to the section in Murph's workbook about knot tying.

"You know I love dogs," said Oscar. "He can sleep in the kennel on the patio. Cadbury never uses it; he snores on our bed all night."

"Oscar, you're a lifesaver. Thank you. I'll collect him tomorrow, once the hospital's released his owner."

"What's he in for?"

"Hypothermia. We found him on Golden Beach again. He'd lit a fire to keep warm."

"Didn't you tell him to stay away from there?"

"We did."

"Hmm. Why would he return? This is all very suspicious. We must rally the troops and digest this latest occurrence."

I plopped Rebel onto the pavement, and Oscar took the end of the makeshift lead.

"What's his name?" he asked.

"Rebel."

"Funny name for a dog. Come on, Rebel. We'll see you tomorrow, Shiraz."

"Thank you so much." I watched them head off along the promenade and marvelled how well Rebel and Cadbury walked together, considering their earlier dislike of each other.

Emily looked up at me as I re-entered the marine rescue building. "Where's the dog?" She bit her bottom lip. "Oh, no. Don't say you couldn't find him. What are we going to tell John?"

"John?"

"His owner. The ambulance crew finally got a name out of him. John Smith. What'll we tell him about his dog?"

"We can tell him that Rebel's safe, well, and settling into his temporary home at Oscar's boarding kennels."

Emily laughed. "Seriously? You gave him to Oscar?"

"Once I'd caught him, yes. But only for the night. I'll visit this John Smith character at the hospital in the morning. I think he owes us an explanation."

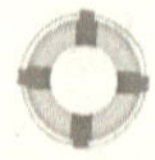

CHAPTER SEVENTEEN

John Smith sat up in bed looking better than I'd ever seen him. The hospital staff had cleaned him, which was probably a shock to his system, fed him a proper meal, which may've been the first he'd enjoyed in a long time and given him clean pyjamas, possibly the first unsoiled clothes he'd worn in decades. He didn't have as much of the odour of a rough sleeper anymore. I wondered why he still wore his large-rimmed, dark sunglasses and decided maybe he had a medical problem with his eyes.

"Where's Rebel?" were his first words as I approached him. His cough hadn't improved, and I allowed him a moment to clear it.

"Rebel's safe. A friend of mine who loves dogs is looking after him. Please don't worry. How are you?"

"Not great. They gave me a bath, which I hated, and they've made me eat this horrible posh food. Beef something-off. They were right about the 'off' part."

I laughed. "Beef Stroganoff?"

"That's it. Why couldn't they give me simple food like a meat pie? None of this foreign rubbish."

I sat on the visitor's chair next to him. "John, what's your fascination with Golden Beach? Why did you return there, when the beach around the landslip's closed?"

"Rebel runs off. Police tape means nothing to him. He can't read, can he?" He laughed, which turned into a guttural coughing fit. "And if he runs under the tape, I have to follow him."

"I'm well aware Rebel likes to run off and be chased. It's his favourite game. So, Rebel ran beneath the tape a second time, you both ended up on Golden Beach under the landslip, but instead of leaving as soon as you'd found him, you decided to gather some wood, light a fire and prepare to spend the night there. Why?"

John scratched the back of his neck and didn't respond.

"And why were you asking my friend in the marine rescue gift shop about the landslip that destroyed Golden Beach settlement? He's the chap who's looking after Rebel, by the way. What's your interest in that event?" I gripped his arm to make him look at me. "What's your secret?"

He turned and sighed. I stayed quiet.

Don't fill his silence, Shiraz. Remember Bill Leonard's reporter trick.

John's face slumped. "I don't have long to live. Terminal lung cancer. There's nothing they can do for me. Weeks, maybe two months, if I'm lucky." He coughed again.

I softened my grip on his arm. "John, I'm so sorry."

"I've had a troubled life," he continued. "I've not been the best person. Ever since I was a teenager, I've been in some kind of bother, in and out of prison. I've never had a stable home. Whenever I've been on the straight and narrow, I've lived rough, or in hostels for people like me."

He paused. "I've never had respect for authority. I take no notice of the police, or anyone. I've done a lot of bad things. I'm not a man you'd bring home to your parents."

"So what brought you to Golden Beach? It wasn't just a convenient place to sleep the night, was it? There's more to it, isn't there?"

He seemed undecided whether to confide in me.

"John, if you need to share something, please talk to me. I'm not police, or authority of any kind. I'm a marine rescue volunteer who wants to make sure you're going to be okay."

"Is Rebel going to be okay?"

"Rebel's probably enjoying a bowl full of food as we speak."

"He's all I've got, you know. I've no idea who'll care for him once I..."

"I'll make sure he's looked after. I promise." I teared up and breathed deeply to compose myself.

"You're one of the first to show me kindness in a long time, Miss. Everyone sees a homeless vagrant. No one wants to know the person."

"You were going to tell me about Golden Beach?" I hoped he was.

John attempted to stifle his cough. "When I was a teenager, my parents were both killed."

"That's terrible. How did it happen? Was it a car accident?"

"An explosion at the factory in Milltown, where they worked. My father died instantly. They took my mother to hospital, and she hung on for a few days, but when she discovered my dad had passed away, she faded away and lost the will to live."

"I'm so sorry. How old were you?"

"Seventeen. Seventeen and an orphan."

"Did you have any brothers or sisters?"

"One sister. She was eighteen, almost nineteen, when it happened. If it hadn't been for her…"

He suffered a noisy coughing fit and took some time to recover.

"After our parents died, we'd no idea what we'd do. We couldn't afford the rent on our house. It was a tiny, two-bedroom terraced place, nothing special, but with only the income from my sister's part-time job at Milltown supermarket, it was a struggle. That's when it began."

"When what began?"

"My life of trouble. I started stealing food. Stealing from shops, restaurants, I even stole from the supermarket where my sister worked, although she never knew at the time. She knew none of my evil deeds. No way I could tell her. My family were good, honest, church-going, working-class folk. 'Thou shalt not steal' and all that. I told her I'd found a job after school to help out, and of course she was overjoyed we had money for groceries. But in reality there was no job, not much school, and no money. Just stealing."

I sighed. This wasn't a world I'd been exposed to. The only wrongdoing I'd seen in London was committed by people who had too much cash and spent some of it on cocaine. That was a regular occurrence; no one thought of it as a crime. Here in Redcliff-upon-Sea, I'd been somehow involved in solving two murders and had even been kidnapped, but I'd never met anyone who'd lived an entire life of illegal activities. I felt sorry for him and the situation he'd been put in, where he felt he had no choice but to steal in order to eat.

"My sister met a man, and they began courting. She was excited, because his family owned a farm, and he clearly had income. She saw him as our ticket out of the situation we found ourselves in. And as she was now eighteen, they could legally be married with no one else's permission. Then my world came crashing down."

"Why? What happened?"

"Someone caught me for the first time." He laughed once. "Certainly not the last time. The store detective at the supermarket grabbed me red handed with a bag full of groceries. I'd become careless, as I hadn't been caught before. I honestly thought I never would be. He dragged me into his office and said he'd call the police. I begged him not to and gave him the story of how my sister and I were orphans, and we had no food. I promised I'd never steal again. Hah! Some promise that was. He said he'd call my sister and ask her to corroborate my tale. Imagine his surprise when I told him she worked there. He dragged her in, and she belted me around the head like our dad used to. She said she was so ashamed; she'd lose her job and then we'd have nothing. My poor sister sat down in that store detective's office and cried her eyes out. I had this funny feeling inside of extreme guilt, yet knowing as soon as this was over, I'd be out stealing again."

I was almost crying myself at this point; John's story was so tragic. I wondered how many other families lived in similar situations and decided I'd never look at a petty thief the same way again.

He continued. "Anyway, it seems the store detective was sweet on my sister. Which was creepy, given that he was around forty and wearing a wedding ring, but he took pity on us and said he wouldn't tell anyone if I promised not to steal again. Like that was going to happen; I just wasn't going to steal from that particular shop anymore. My sister thanked him; she even kissed him on the cheek, which I reckon made his day. But this episode made her even more determined to marry this chap she'd met. The following day, she told me she was meeting his parents to tell them they were getting married."

I froze, as I realised how the skeleton in the car, Bill Leonard's tale from forty-seven years ago and John Smith's story all might intertwine. But I needed to double confirm they were definitely related to the same events.

"What happened when your sister met the parents? They must've been overjoyed about the forthcoming wedding."

"Exactly the opposite. Apparently, his father said they'd be getting married over his dead body. Clearly, he didn't like her for some reason."

Bingo. Exactly as Bill Leonard related.

"Wow," I said. "That seems an old-fashioned, extreme reaction."

"Yes, but there was no way my sister was going to let this chap go. He had a steady income, and maybe even some savings. She told him she loved him; she didn't want to live without him, and they should get married even though his parents didn't want them to. That was all a story. I don't think she loved him at all; she needed the security for herself and me. The next thing I knew, I was being dressed up in some horrible, borrowed clothes and dragged to a room near the council offices along with my sister, her friend from the supermarket and this man of hers. They were married there by a bloke in a suit. There was one other chap at the wedding, some friend of the groom. I remember him because he slipped away back to our street and decorated the groom's car for a joke. He covered it in balloons and spray painted 'Just Married' on it. I thought that was hilarious."

John coughed so loudly, I was surprised none of the staff arrived to check on him. He recovered and continued.

"Anyway, a reporter from the Milltown newspaper took a photo of us in front of the car, then my sister's new man slipped a fifty pound note in my hand. I stared at it. I'd never seen a fifty before."

"Her husband gave you money?"

"Yep. A whole fifty pounds. That was a lot back in those days. Still is to many people. He told me to use it to buy food and pay the rent for the week. He said he was taking my sister south, and they'd send for me in a few days. All I could think about was what I was going to do with that fifty. I'd already planned an evening buying beer and cigarettes, maybe go to the nightclub in the town centre. I wasn't thinking as far ahead as rent and food." He laughed again. "My sister kissed me and said she'd see me soon. Then they climbed into his car, decorated with all that stuff, and…"

His voice faltered.

"And what, John?"

He turned to me, and tears ran from the bottom of his sunglasses. "And that was the last time I saw her."

CHAPTER EIGHTEEN

John Smith suffered another coughing fit, and his entire body shook.

I waited for him to compose himself, then asked, "John, what was your sister's name?"

"Mary. She was called Mary."

The pieces of the puzzle were coming together. I was fairly sure I knew where his sister was, but I didn't think I should be the one to tell him about her death.

"It's a tragic story, John. But it doesn't explain why you came to Redcliff-upon-Sea. Why did you think she'd be here?"

"A week after the wedding, I received a letter. I tore it open excitedly, hoping it contained another fifty pounds for me. But there was no money in it. Just a note. It looked like her handwriting, but I'd never paid attention at school, and I couldn't read well. I asked a neighbour to read it for me. The neighbour told me the letter said she was living by the sea in the South, and she'd send funds for me to join her as soon as she could save up. It didn't give an address or even the name of the town where she'd settled. Naturally, I was excited to have heard from her, and I stuffed the letter in the envelope and kept it. The days dragged on and, every morning, I stood outside our house waiting for the postman. After another week, a second letter arrived. But this wasn't handwritten; it was typed."

John coughed relentlessly, and I wondered if I should call a nurse.

He took shallow breaths, then continued. "The same neighbour read it for me. It was addressed to my parents, and stated if they didn't pay the rent up to date, we'd be thrown out. The meaning of this passed me by, as I was living on my wits, stealing food again. I even stole money, but I didn't think to use it to pay the landlord; I bought cigarettes and alcohol. After another few weeks, some men knocked on the door. They said they were taking back the house, and I had to get out. I told them about my parents passing, and my sister moving away, then one of them asked how old I was because, if I was a child, he'd have to call the Social Services. At that point, I scarpered with the clothes on my back, my stolen money and my sister's letter in my pocket and nothing else. I never even stopped to think about how any other letters from her would find me."

I waited while he coughed and asked him again how he came to find Golden Beach.

"I kept that letter from my sister with me always," he said. "It was our only connection; I had nothing else to remind me of her. My career progressed from stealing food and money to stealing cars. I heard the police were on my tail, so I went on the run and moved to the East End of London, where I changed my name and hid for a while. Through my contacts there, I found a job working for a man who altered cars' identities and resold them once I'd stolen them. Naturally, the law caught up with us, and I had to flee again. To cut a long story short, after a lifetime of escaping justice, I woke up last month in the latest of a string of doss houses. I was coughing continually, and I collapsed after breakfast. They called an ambulance and, following tests, I discovered I had lung cancer. It's not surprising, after the way I've treated my body all my life."

He paused, covered his mouth and coughed violently. "By the time I found out, it was too late. That was four weeks ago. When I knew I had a short time to live, my thoughts returned to finding my sister. I knew she'd be 65 years old, so the chances were, she'd still be alive. A kindly nurse at the hospital listened to my story, like you are now. She asked me if I had the original letter, and I told her I'd always kept it. That nice lady read it to me, the same as that neighbour all those years previously. She said it was a shame my sister hadn't included her address. As she replaced it in the envelope, she noticed a mark across the stamp."

"A postmark?"

"That's what she called it, Miss. She told me this mark said 'Redcliff-upon-Sea'. We looked at a map together, and she pointed out where Redcliff was. You might not believe this, but I'd never seen a map of England before. I said I wanted to go to Redcliff and try to track down my sister while I was well enough. Before I..., before it was too late for me. I packed up my things, not that I owned much. Then she looked me in the eye and said, 'You can't go by yourself'. I was overjoyed, and grinned from ear to ear as I imagined she'd say she was coming with me. But she didn't. Instead, she said her next-door neighbour had a dog they couldn't look after anymore. And would I like a companion? I'd always liked dogs, though I'd never had one myself. That's how Rebel came into my life. This nurse drove me and my new pet to the train station. She bought me a ticket to Redcliff with her own money and made sure I boarded the right train. Some people are angels, aren't they, Miss? That lady was one, and I'm thinking you might be one too."

I didn't want John to think of me as one of his guardian angels. I needed to work out how he tied in with Mary's death, or even her murder.

"So you arrived in Redcliff-upon-Sea, and then what?"

"I slept rough at the train station until the staff threatened to call the police. I asked them if anyone knew a Mary Smith, but they didn't. The man she'd married was called Patrick, but I didn't know his surname, which would've been her married name. No one had heard of any couple called Patrick and Mary in Redcliff. Eventually, I ended up at the museum on a freezing afternoon when I was searching for somewhere to keep warm. A kindly lady in the gift shop let me in for free, and I wandered around the displays. As I walked from room to room, I came across the exhibit about the Golden Beach landslip and, to my surprise, there was the wedding photo of my sister and her new husband, with his car, as I remembered it all those years ago. And it gave me hope. Because the newspaper said they were missing. Not dead. My sister could be alive somewhere. Maybe even still here in Redcliff?"

He coughed again and closed his eyes, and I realised this outpouring had exhausted him. I wrestled with my conscience and my moral responsibility. The chances were his sister's decomposed body was lying in a morgue and subject to a police investigation. But I didn't have enough information yet, and it wasn't my job to tell him.

I leant forward and held his arm. "John, I'll help you find her. Whatever it takes."

"You will? D'you think she's alive?"

"I don't know. But I'll start asking around. Maybe someone here remembers her?"

A young nurse in a white uniform stopped by the bedside. "Good morning, Mr Smith." He nodded a greeting at me. "How are you feeling today?"

"Not great," said John. "Tired." He spluttered into his hand.

"I'm sure," said the nurse. "You've had a nasty experience. It's time for me to check your readings." The nurse wrapped a blood pressure cuff around his upper arm, and a machine attached to it began beeping. He took his temperature with a similar device to the one Karam the paramedic had used the previous day. "Mr Smith, the doctor's asked if we could take blood for tests. Would you let me do that?"

"Will it hurt?"

"Only a scratch. It'll be over before you know it."

"All right. If you have to."

The nurse swabbed the inside of his elbow, screwed a small tube onto the end of a needle and inserted it.

I stood. "John, I have to go now, but I'll come back and see you again."

"Will you bring Rebel?"

"They won't let him into the hospital. You'll have to wait until you're discharged before you can see him. But I assure you, he's in the best hands."

"Thank you, Miss. He means everything to me. He's all I have until I find Mary."

Emily was relaxing at our flat, reading a book on the couch with Boots curled up on her lap. Sunday was the only day the café closed, and I knew she treasured these moments, so I slipped in and opened the fridge, wondering what to have for lunch.

"Hi, Shiraz," she said. Her book shut, and Boots' paws pa-doomphed onto the floor. "Where've you been this morning?"

"At the hospital, visiting John Smith." Boots smooched around my legs and miaowed loudly. "Boots, I'm not opening the fridge for you. Sorry. Your dinner's still hours away."

"John Smith?" asked Emily. "Why did you go to see him? Smelly old tramp."

"I was curious. Why does he keep returning to Golden Beach? Why is he so obsessed by the place? And he related a long story."

"Ooh, I love stories. Shall I make lunch and you can tell me about it? Are yesterday's café leftovers okay?"

I laughed. "Of course. What've you got? I'll boil the kettle."

"Filled rolls or a meat pie."

The thought of John's preference of meat pies over beef something-off made me smile to myself.

"Where to start with John Smith?" I said, as Emily pulled containers from the fridge.

"D'you think that's his real name?"

"Why wouldn't it be?"

"John Smith's a generic name. It's like he made it up."

"There must be people christened John Smith. Anyway, get this, it turns out he's Mary's younger brother."

"Mary, the skeleton in the car, Mary?"

"One and the same."

"Wow. That explains his obsession with the location, I guess."

"Yes, but he doesn't know what's happened to her. He came to Redcliff to find her, as he hadn't seen her since they were teenagers, and he didn't know about the landslip or anything."

"How tragic, to have come all this way and then find out she died decades ago."

"He doesn't know she's dead at all. Their last communication was a letter from her when he was seventeen."

"Are you going to tell him?"

"Not yet. For one, I don't think it's my place to release information about a deceased person to their relatives."

"Quite right. Murph told me if we ever find a body during marine rescue, we must let the police break the news to the family."

"Right. The other thing is, we're not sure the body in the car is Mary, are we?"

"It has to be. She went missing after the disaster, and a skeleton of a woman turns up in a subsequent landslip in the same make of car as the one in her wedding photo. It couldn't be anyone else."

I rubbed my chin.

"Oh, no," said Emily, placing a plate in front of me. "What are you thinking?"

"I know how we could tell for certain the body's Mary's."

CHAPTER NINETEEN

Emily sat at the table. "How could we tell the body's definitely Mary?" she asked me.

"If John Smith's her brother, he could take a DNA test, and it could be compared with the skeleton."

"This is way out of our league, Shiraz. Shall we visit Oscar and ask his opinion?"

"Definitely. I wonder how Rebel's getting on? I promised John he was being well cared for."

Oscar was tending his vegetable garden. Or at least attempting to, while Rebel charged around the plot chasing Cadbury in circles.

"Looks like Cadbury has a new playmate." Emily giggled as they somersaulted over each other.

"I'm trying to rake the earth flat to plant spring seeds," said Oscar, bracing himself as the dogs crashed against his legs and tore off again, "but these two keep digging it up. Cadbury's never been so active."

"I'm pleased they've made friends," I said, as they raced past again. "Would you like a break? We need your opinion on something."

"Of course." Oscar removed his gardening shoes and led us into his kitchen. "My wife's out at a church service. The season of Lent. Forty days of us going without biscuits, cakes and dessert. Forty days of hell, if you ask me."

We laughed.

"I've brought some cake from the café with me," said Emily. "We'd better make sure there are no crumbs for her to find."

"Excellent," said Oscar. "It'll taste all the better for being contraband." He switched on the kettle and pulled three mugs from a cupboard.

"Here's the big news." I slid out a chair and sat at his kitchen table. "The man who owns the dog ripping around your garden claims to be the brother of the girl who died in the car."

"On what basis?" asked Oscar. "Did he see the newspaper article with the photo of the car being recovered? When there's an unexplained death, a heap of claimants come out of the woodwork. Some of them want reflected attention; maybe some think there'll be an inheritance. I'd be suspicious of his supposed relationship."

"He wouldn't have seen the article, because he can't read. But he told me a long story which made sense. They grew up in the North, and an accident killed their parents when he and his sister were both teenagers. His sister married a man who she hoped would lift them out of their poverty; he's the chap in the wedding photo at the museum. But he stole her away to Golden Beach decades ago and left John behind."

"John?"

"John Smith. The brother. The scruffy man who owns Rebel. And he never saw her again."

"He couldn't have, anyway," said Emily. "Because she was dead."

"Right. But he doesn't know that."

"If he took a DNA test, it would prove they were brother and sister," said Oscar.

"My thoughts exactly. How do we arrange that?"

"Easy. Inform the police we've found the brother of the deceased and ask them to arrange a DNA test to confirm his statement. They'd have to tell him she's passed away at the same time, though. Where is he?"

"Still in Redcliff and Alnchurch Hospital."

Oscar placed steaming mugs of tea in front of us, and Emily opened the cake tin. I peeked in and saw a Victoria Sponge, with whipped cream squishing out of the sides and a snowing of icing sugar on top. She'd just cut the first slice when a crash came from outside, followed by barking. Oscar paused, shook his head and elected to ignore it. "You'll be interested to hear this, too. I've heard back from my old friend in pathology. The toxicology report concluded the poisonous substance in her body was arsenic."

"Why would she have arsenic in her? That's definitely murder, right? No one would voluntarily take arsenic."

"The pathologist said it could potentially have been an overdose. He told me arsenic is used in medicine, specifically in a product called"—he referred to his notepad—"Melarsoprol. It's used for treatment of tropical diseases in a hospital situation only. He also said, because she died decades ago, we can't be sure whether she was dead when the landslip covered the car, or whether she died after it buried her."

"To be honest," said Emily, "I hope for her sake she died of poisoning or a broken neck, rather than being smothered by the landslip. That sounds like a terrible way to die. Do we have any other clues?"

"I thought you didn't want to investigate this death?" I prodded her in fun. "But this may or may not be a clue." I felt in my pocket and showed the glass bottle to them. "What d'you reckon it is?"

"It's a glass bottle," said Emily. "A very dirty one."

"Thank you, Captain Obvious. I mean, what was it used for?"

She took the bottle from me and twisted it around. "Where did you find this?"

"On the beach where we discovered John and Rebel. At the base of the landslip."

"Hmm," she said, holding it up to the light. "It reminds me of the milk bottles we used to be given at school. My dad used to keep a row of these in his shed to store bits and bobs." She turned it upside down to see if there was anything embossed on the bottom. "It's definitely old; there's nothing like it these days. And it looks like it's been burnt, from the black discolouration."

Oscar cradled his mug and bit his bottom lip. "What do we have here? Do we have a murder? We have a body." He shook his head. "This is hard, because of the passage of time. We need more information, more evidence."

"What about Bill Leonard's story?" I asked. "Or, better still, his photos. They might tell us something. I'm going to Headland Bay library tomorrow to meet him so he can show them to me."

"I need to go to the wholesaler tomorrow afternoon," said Emily. "I'm nearly out of everything. Self-raising flour, eggs, kitchen towels, floor cleaning fluid, teabags. Would you like a lift?"

"Yes, please. That'd be preferable to chasing the once-a-day bus. So long as there's room for me in your car with all your purchases."

Oscar rubbed his chin. "While you two do that, I'll have a chat with the police and see if they can persuade your John Smith to submit to a DNA test. Unfortunately, he'll find out his sister's probably been dead since the 1970s, but he has to discover that sometime, and the police should be the ones telling him."

A cacophony of barks and the sound of broken pottery came from the garden. "That's my cue to get back out there," said Oscar. "Let's regroup tomorrow."

I lay in bed that Sunday evening and hugged myself.

Being single had its advantages. I didn't have to answer to anyone else's agenda. I could go out whenever I wanted to, come home whenever I wanted to, and meet up with whoever I wanted to, without discovering my husband was meeting up with his real soulmate. His lifelong love. The one that wasn't me.

But being a couple had felt comfortable. Sharing precious, intimate, familiar moments. Sitting opposite someone at a restaurant and knowing exactly what they were going to order before they opened the menu. Knowing your partner's favourite shops, favourite wine, favourite slippers. I needed someone who I could be myself with.

Was it too soon? Did I need time to heal first, before I rushed headlong into the wrong relationship? Again.

Scenes of Karam playing the lead in a Bollywood movie swarmed through my mind. I imagined him dressed in flowing robes, a sword at his side, riding up on a groomed, white stallion and sweeping me into his arms, rescuing me from imminent peril. Saving me from a charging elephant, perhaps, or giant snakes. Yes! Snakes. Karam arrives on his pure-white horse, slices the head off a writhing viper that's about to bite me, then, with one arm, he pulls me up into the saddle behind him, and we gallop off into the sunset.

I grinned at the fanciful image, and wondered if, right now, he was racing with lights and sirens to the scene of a car accident, the modern-day version of my fantasy.

Then there was Adam. Adam, the tall, hunky, Coastguard man who really had rescued me from Golden Beach landslip. I couldn't see how he'd be interested in me. I was a part-time volunteer who couldn't stop getting into trouble and needing help, never mind being able to save anyone else.

And then there was David.

David, who'd first caught my eye when I joined Redcliff Marine Rescue. Emily and he had shown interest in each other, but that didn't show signs of progressing. Although he was more her age. Definitely too young for me.

I needed a more mature man.

Like Karam.

Or Adam.

Aaaarrrgggghhh.

Bill Leonard sat in his usual seat in the library. I wondered if the other patrons knew it was Bill's spot, or whether they were avoiding him, as the area contained four chairs, but no one occupied the others.

He looked up and grunted. "Nothing good in the paper these days. No quality reporting. Can you believe this?" He jabbed his finger so hard at his newspaper I thought he'd poke it through.

"What's the matter?"

"This title." He flapped the paper in front of him, folded it and turned it to show me. "D'you see what's wrong?"

I scanned the headline, which announced 'Council to review funding for biannual flower festival.' I couldn't see anything amiss. "Sorry, Bill, I don't have a journalist's background like you do. What's the problem?"

"Biannual." Bill stabbed at the offending word. "Biannual means twice a year. They don't have the flower festival twice a year. It's every two years. The correct word is 'biennial'. A good reporter should know better. Then, in the article's body, it says, 'The Council has two choices, neither of which will please everyone.' They don't have two choices. They have one choice, and two options. Can nobody write correct English?"

I sat opposite and waited for him to calm down. "Bill, maybe you should take a break from reading the paper? I was wondering if I could see those photos you mentioned last week? The ones of the landslip the paper wouldn't publish."

He sat forward and spoke conspiratorially. "Shh. Not so loud. Walls have ears. Here's what we'll do. You go over to the bookshelves and pretend to be searching for a title. Meanwhile, I'll leave the library. Count to one hundred slowly, then follow me, and we'll meet at the corner of the street by the White Lion pub. We've been seen leaving the library together once. We mustn't again. People will wonder what we're up to."

"Um, okay," I stage-whispered back, thinking this was all rather Graham Greene. "Who are you concerned about?"

"Trust me," he said mysteriously, so I shrugged, stood and walked over to the bookshelves. As I pretended to scan through mysteries by Agatha Christie and Ngaio Marsh, from the corner of my eye I watched Bill push himself to his feet, collect his bag and walking stick and hobble to the exit. I counted to one hundred as instructed, then followed.

"Ready?" he asked once I'd caught up with him. "My street's opposite."

We crossed the main thoroughfare and entered a tree-lined avenue. Pleasant, detached houses bordered the road, with well-kept front gardens. A middle-aged man pruning roses waved and called out to Bill, but Bill pretended not to hear him and walked on with his head down.

As soon as we were out of earshot, I asked him, "Why didn't you greet that man? And why the big secrecy in leaving the library?"

"I told you, this landslip of yours at Golden Beach holds a secret. And if people around here see us together, they might think we're digging up old bones."

"Why would they think that, Bill? I don't have a police uniform, or anything."

"You could be plain clothes. A detective. Or a private investigator. Nothing stays confidential around here for long."

I smiled to myself and decided to humour him. We reached the front gate of a small bungalow with an overgrown garden. He opened the front door, and the smell of mothballs immediately assaulted my nostrils. The floral furniture covers reminded me of a Laura Ashley catalogue.

"Here," he said. "Have a seat. Make yourself comfortable."

I moved a pile of old magazines and sat.

"Right," said Bill. "Golden Beach landslide photos." He opened a filing cabinet and pulled out a thick folder, then surprised me by passing me a pair of white gloves, the kind a butler in a stately home might use. "Put these on." He tugged on another pair. "We need to be careful handling these artefacts."

I pulled on the gloves which felt soft against my skin, like thin exercise socks. Inside the folder, layers of tissue paper separated A4-sized black-and-white photos. I peeled the protective covering back and held up the first one. Although the scene was clearly the aftermath of a disaster, I found it hard to tell who the rescuers were and who were the rescued. They both wore filthy clothes, and mud covered their hands and faces.

"Look at the next one," said Bill. "It's more dramatic."

I slipped the first photo carefully back into the paper and turned to the second. It depicted houses smashed at the bottom of a cliff, windows broken, curtains hanging out. One bungalow's roof had detached in one piece and sat next to three of the four walls, which appeared surreal.

I shook my head slowly. "The nearest thing I've seen to these pictures is articles in the news about earthquakes. I'm amazed your editor wouldn't publish them."

"He did publish that one. What he wouldn't print was the story of the missing people."

I flipped to the next photo, which showed the section of road from Redcliff-upon-Sea to Headland Bay collapsed into the sea, as if a sea monster had helped itself to a giant bite of tarmac. The following picture was a close up of people standing next to an old truck.

"That's Tommy Colstead's truck," said Bill. "We ferried people to the hospital in it. Very useful."

The last image depicted a group huddled around a fire, wrapped in blankets. In the background, people drank tea and ate food from a makeshift trestle table.

"That's the aftermath," said Bill. "Like a war zone complete with refugees."

I held the photo in both gloved hands and turned it towards the light coming from Bill's window.

The woman tending to the injured looked familiar.

CHAPTER TWENTY

"Is that Violet Farmer?" I asked Bill, pointing at the photo. "This person in uniform among the group of nurses, bandaging the man's shoulder."

He took the photo from me and turned it over, but nothing written on the back identified her. "I don't know Violet Farmer," he said. "Is she a friend of yours?"

"She works at the museum. She told me she helped look after the injured." I peered at the picture again. "Maybe it's not her."

"She's not the missing woman, is she? I would've spotted that."

"No. She's not Mary Hebblethwaite. She looks nothing like her. Could I take a copy of this, please?"

"Of course," said Bill. He watched me hold my phone over the picture and raised his eyebrows at the sound of a camera shutter coming from it. "I still can't understand how these new-fangled things work. When I was a reporter, we had thirty-six pictures to a film, and we needed to use the entire film before we could see if our images were any good. Nowadays, you young things take as many photos as you like. Snap, snap, snap. Pictures of yourselves, your pets, even your food. If I'd entered a restaurant in the 1970s, pulled out my close-up lens and photographed my prawn cocktail, people would've thought I was nuts."

I laughed. "Yep. It's a bit much, isn't it? I'm 38, and I can remember my parents using film cameras."

"This is another you'll be interested in," said Bill. He slid over the photo of the wedding; the one in the newspaper cutting. Bill's original hadn't been cropped, and it showed all four people and the Triumph Spitfire behind them. Besides the missing bride and groom, a bridesmaid stood next to Mary, and a short man in an ill-fitting suit stood alongside Patrick. I presumed he was the best man.

"The car number plate's clearer in this, isn't it?" said Bill, holding up the photo with his gloved hand. "But it's terribly tiny. Why don't you take a picture of this one too?"

"Good idea. I can zoom in and try to read it."

As I snapped the picture, my phone rang, and I answered it.

"Hi, Emily. I'm still at Bill's house. Could you pick me up outside the library in ten minutes? Thanks. Bye."

I turned to Bill, who clearly hoped I'd stay for afternoon tea and conversation. "Bill, that's my lift back to Redcliff. I must be going."

"Shame," he said. "We could've discussed this mystery for ages. Would you leave me your phone number in case I think of anything else you might be interested in?"

"Of course. You're welcome to call me. I'd love to get to the bottom of what happened at Golden Beach."

Emily swerved the Morris Minor to the kerb as I stood outside the library. Spits of rain blobbed onto the pavement.

"Could we please put the car roof up this afternoon?" I asked. "I don't want to get wet."

"Aw," said Emily. "It's not raining properly."

I pointed at dark-grey clouds further along the coast, looming over Redcliff-upon-Sea. "It'll rain hard before we make it home."

"All right, we'll pull over to raise it when it starts."

I puffed hard and plopped into the passenger seat. She pushed the stick into first gear, disengaged the handbrake, and we pulled away.

"You're quiet," she said, as we exited the town boundaries, and the Morris Minor reached its maximum speed. The gears crunched as she changed into fourth while rounding a bend.

"Sorry." I turned to her and smiled. "I was miles away."

"Were you on Golden Beach, by any chance?"

"Yes. Reflecting on what Bill Leonard told me."

"You were there for a while."

"The poor chap's lonely. He wanted to hang on to my company as long as possible." I pulled my phone from my pocket and inspected the photo of the wedding couple.

"So much sadness." I shook my head.

"Sadness?"

"Sadness. Sadness that a young couple couldn't obtain their parents' blessing to marry because of a bigoted father's opinion of their different religions. Not even different religions. They were both Christians, for goodness' sake. Different parts of the same belief." I thumped the dashboard. "How could anyone be so callous?"

"Hey," said Emily. "Don't hurt my car. Say sorry."

I rolled my eyes and stroked the Morris's dashboard. "Sorry, car. But d'you see my point? My father was from a Muslim family, although he wasn't exactly devout. My mother didn't have a religious bone in her body. But they still married with no objections."

"So what d'you reckon?" asked Emily. "The Hebblethwaites ended up at Golden Beach because they ran away to be married? Patrick must've stormed out of his parents' house after the argument, taken Mary and driven south. I don't know why they chose Golden Beach, though."

"They weren't married in Golden Beach." I turned the photo of the wedding car towards her. "This photo shows them in front of a terrace of red-brick houses; the kind you see in northern mining towns. There are no streets like that around here; everything's built of the local stone or those painted, wooden boards."

Emily stared at the photo.

"Watch out!" I cried, grabbing the wheel to keep her car on the correct side of the white lines. She slowed down as we entered Alnchurch and turned left to join the Redcliff road.

"And what's odd," I said, "is Oscar's mention of the poison. We don't, of course, know it was definitely Mary who'd met her end in that way. If Oscar persuades the police to take John Smith's DNA, it might prove it one way or another."

"But everything points to her," said Emily. "The couple had a blue Triumph, the car and them both went missing the night of the storm, the autopsy ages the skeleton at around twenty years at the time of death. Isn't that how old John Smith said his sister was?"

"She was eighteen." I stared out of the window as dusk fell, and I rubbed my hands together.

"Uh-oh," said Emily. "What are you thinking now?"

I turned and patted her left arm, which rested on the gearstick. "I'm thinking I need a trip to Hebble Bridge."

"Hebble Bridge?" Emily turned her head and stared at me. "What will you discover going up there after all these decades? There won't be anyone who remembers two young people who ran away to get married and disappeared almost fifty years ago."

"I'm sure you're right. But there's no harm in looking. Would you come with me?"

"How could I? The café's open six days a week. Hebble Bridge is at the other end of the country. Even if we left after Saturday afternoon closing, we'd never be back by Sunday night. We'd need another day."

"Isn't it a public holiday on Monday?"

"Um, yes."

"Do you open on public holidays?"

"Only in the summer."

"How about after the café closes on Saturday, we head off and drive north? We'll arrive late Saturday evening, check into a guest house, spend Sunday investigating and return to Redcliff on Monday."

"There's no way this old car will survive a trip that long. She just about makes it to Headland Bay and back."

"All right, we'll take the train."

"But how will I get the café ready for the next week? I need four hours to do that."

"I'll help you. If we work hard together, it'll only be two hours."

Emily puffed hard. "Shiraz, you certainly can be persuasive. But I'm sorry. I can't spend my entire weekend on a wild duck chase, return completely exhausted and then have a full week's work in the café. Not happening."

CHAPTER TWENTY-ONE

The sleek, modern train swooshed through flat, featureless countryside. I stared out of the window as fields and farms flashed past in the Saturday afternoon gloom.

"Why?" asked Emily from her seat opposite. "Why do I always end up doing what you want me to do? I'm trying to pretend I'm going on a fancy holiday somewhere, rather than investigating the appearance of a skeleton belonging to someone I didn't know, who died in a car I've never seen before."

"Emily, where's your sense of adventure? Have you ever visited the North?"

"I don't think so. Maybe, if I shut my eyes, I can pretend the whooshing of the train is the wind outside my cosy bedroom above the café."

I'd researched Hebble Bridge and discovered the station where Bill Leighton alighted forty-seven years previously had closed, and new owners had transformed the ticket office into a railway-themed tearoom called 'The Dining Carriage'. The nearest train station was now in Milltown, several miles away, so I'd arranged to rent a small car on our arrival. It was night when we arrived, and Emily didn't seem entirely comfortable driving an unfamiliar vehicle after dark in the rain.

"Why don't you drive?" she asked, as soon as she sat in the driver's seat and stared at the flat screens which formed the instrument cluster. "I've no idea how to operate these modern cars. They're like spaceships."

"I'm not driving because I can't find my driving licence, remember? I haven't used it since I left London, and I haven't missed it at all."

Emily felt around the steering column. "This car doesn't have a key either. How on earth d'you start a car without a key?"

"Push the button. The round one that says 'start'."

"I'm pushing it. Nothing's happening."

"Is the brake depressed?"

"The only one who's depressed is me. This is too hard. Why can't cars be simple like my Morris Minor?"

"Push the brake pedal and press the button."

"Okay, I'm pushing the brake. At least, I think it's the brake. And I've pressed the button. Oh, here we go. The screen's lit up. But I can't hear the engine, can you?"

I turned my head to one side and agreed I couldn't hear an engine.

"Maybe it's really quiet because it's brand new," said Emily. "I'll lean out of the window and listen."

"They're electric windows. Push that button." I pointed at the window control.

"Everything's electric, isn't it? The instruments, the start button, the window. This whole car's electric."

"Emily, you've got it."

"I have?"

"What you said. The whole car's electric."

She frowned at me. "Yes, and?"

"The whole car's electric. It's an electric car. That's why you can't hear the engine."

Once we'd established that this vehicle was as futuristic to Emily as the *Starship Enterprise*, we drove gingerly away from the railway station. I'd booked a bed-and-breakfast in Milltown. Close enough to Hebble Bridge for the action, not so close that we didn't have an escape if anything turned ugly. Not that I expected anything to turn ugly, but we were about to insert ourselves into what was rapidly looking like a forty-seven-year-old unsolved murder, and I'd no idea what we'd unearth once we started digging.

Father Dermot O'Leary inspected me over his glasses as we accosted him leaving the Church of the Holy Assumption the following morning. His shock of white hair swept luxuriously back from his forehead, as if he'd recently been hanging out of a speeding car's window.

"Genealogists, are you? Goodness, we seem to have a lot of them. It's become a fascination with people, tracing their family trees. I had a chap last week who was a computer whizz; he showed me some programme where you send away a drop of your blood, and they tell from it who you're related to; people you've never even heard of." He shook his head slowly. "Whatever will they think of next? How can I help you young ladies?"

"We're looking for a family with the surname Hebblethwaite."

"That won't be hard," said the priest. "There are several Hebblethwaites around here. Two of them were in church not half-an-hour ago."

"Specifically," I continued, "a man called Patrick Hebblethwaite, who also had a son named Patrick. I reckon the younger man would be in his sixties or seventies, if he's still alive. The older one would almost certainly be dead. But I know he was living here in 1976."

"I've been the priest here for fifteen years, and I don't know a father and son both called Patrick Hebblethwaite, so we'll need to turn to the parish records. Come into the rectory."

We followed him into a house next door to the church, and he showed us into a study. A dark, wooden desk stood in the centre, and he invited us to sit in two high-backed chairs opposite it. A clock ticked slowly, then chimed the hour.

Father O'Leary lifted the lid of a window seat and tugged out a leather-bound book. "These days, this is all on computers but, in the 1970s, it was still recorded by hand," he explained, as he flopped it open on his desk.

He ran his eyes down the first page, then licked his finger and turned to the next one. "What year did you say? 1976?"

"Yes, or afterwards."

"Here. Patrick Hebblethwaite. Died 2nd April 1976, aged seventy. It says he left a wife called Eileen, and a son also called Patrick, so I reckon we've found our chap, don't you?"

"I'd say so. I wonder if Eileen's death is recorded in your book too?"

He flicked the page and hummed to himself as he scanned it. "Here she is. Oh. That's unusual. She passed away on the same day, aged sixty-nine."

"They must've perished in a car accident," said Emily.

I pushed out my bottom lip. "Maybe." I turned to the Priest. "Would you have marriage records as well? We're interested in the marriage of this younger Patrick Hebblethwaite to a person called Mary Smith."

"Were they married at this church?"

"No," I said. "Although Patrick may have lived in the parish, I think they were married at a registry office."

"Registry office, eh?" said the Priest. "Now why would they have done that, when the Hebblethwaites were obviously a good Catholic family? Were either of the couple divorced? If so, the church wouldn't have married them."

"Not that we know of. We believe his wife was a protestant."

"Protestant? No wonder they were married in a registry office. For a Catholic to marry a protestant, they'd probably have needed to obtain special permission from the bishop, which wasn't always straightforward."

"If they were forced to marry in a registry office, where would they be likely to go?"

"The only registry office around here's in Milltown, next to the council buildings. Now, if you'll excuse me, I have a baptism to prepare for. Another little one coming to faith."

"Thank you, Father. Thank you for all your help."

"God be with you in your search for your family members. Go in peace." He showed us out.

Amen to that, I thought.

"Now what?" asked Emily.

"Now we find the registry office."

"It won't be open. It's Sunday lunchtime."

"At least let's discover where it is. We can see if it looks like the wedding photo. Then we'll know we're on the right track."

To our surprise, the registry office was open, although it was in a detached building surrounded by municipal gardens, which looked nothing like the street in the photo with the balloon-adorned Triumph Spitfire. A couple aged around fifty emerged, the woman in a smart off-white outfit, the man in a cheap suit. Other similarly dressed people followed them.

"Probably a second marriage," said Emily. "You can tell by the clothes."

"If I ever get married a second time, I'll wear a white, flowing Stella McCartney design. Like I did when I married Monty. But a more up-to-date version, without a bow."

"Gosh, you do have it all planned. Um, are you planning on getting married again?"

My mind briefly flashed to Karam, and I wondered whether it was acceptable for a Sikh to marry a non-Sikh, half-Muslim, and whether a non-Sikh, half-Muslim bride would be permitted to wear a white Stella McCartney dress to walk up the aisle. And whether Sikh temples even had aisles.

"I'm not marrying anyone today, Emily. We have a mystery to solve first."

She giggled, and we entered.

"Hi." I addressed a woman who was packing papers into a briefcase. "Do you hold information about marriages here? We're genealogists, tracing family history."

The lady inspected us with her lips pursed and her eyes slitted. "Genealogists should be familiar with the Birth, Deaths and Marriages bureau who hold the records for this region. We don't keep any here."

Emily blushed. "Oh, um. We're new to this. Thanks for the tip." She grabbed my hand and tugged me outside onto the lawn, while the woman watched us suspiciously.

"Shiraz, will you stop dragging me into situations?" Emily waved her arms in the air. "This is a dead end. Patrick Hebblethwaite's parents are dead. Patrick's probably dead.

Mary's dead. Can we please stop all this nonsense and go home?"

"Shh." I clutched her shoulder and turned her away from the wedding party, whose video was being overdubbed by Emily yelling in the background.

She twisted out of my grip. "Don't shush me. What have we achieved coming here? Nothing. This is all a wild duck chase."

"Goose."

"Goose yourself."

"Not you. The expression is a 'wild goose chase', not a 'wild duck chase'."

"Whatever. I'm going back to our bed-and-breakfast, changing my clothes and popping out to find something for dinner. You can join me, but only if you stop going on about landslips, skeletons and events from forty-seven years ago." She marched over to the rental car, opened the door and flopped into the driver's seat.

I half expected her to drive away, but the car remained parked at the side of the road. Cautiously, I opened the passenger door and poked my head in. "Not going without me, then?"

Emily clenched her teeth. "I would, but I can't start it."

Once I'd reminded Emily to push the brake pedal and press the start button, we followed the satnav's directions away from the municipal gardens, along a dual carriageway, then through roads of diminishing width. Trees no longer graced the pavements. Cars parked on both sides of the streets of terraced, red-brick houses caused Emily consternation as she navigated the narrow gaps between them.

"This isn't the right way," said Emily. "I don't recognise this at all. We needed to stick to the main road, but this is a residential area."

I pulled my phone from my pocket, swiped it open and scrolled the screen.

"What are you doing?" asked Emily. "Are you opening Google Maps? Because this satnav's directions are definitely misleading."

"I'm not," I said. "Look at this." I showed her my phone.

"Shiraz, will you stop showing me that photo of the couple with the wedding car? I told you; don't go on about events forty-seven years ago. We're not talking about that subject anymore."

"But look." I pointed out of the windscreen and then showed her the phone again. She tried to inspect it and braked hard in the middle of the street.

"What? I can't drive and study your stupid picture at the same time. What?"

I indicated a tall structure in the distance. "That factory tower. The red-brick one ahead of us. D'you see it?"

"Yes. So?"

"Don't you get it? Look at the photo on my phone. Here, I'll blow up this section." I enlarged the image with two fingers and showed her.

She gasped. "Is it the same one?" Her gaze wavered between the phone and the view through the windscreen.

"Yep. I reckon so. We're on the very street where this picture was taken. Park here." I pointed. "Where that Mini came out."

"I'll never fit this car into that space."

"You will. See this button here?" I pointed at a control in the car depicting a symbol of a steering wheel with the letter 'P' next to it. "If you line up the car next to the space and push that, it'll park itself."

"Seriously?" Emily's eyes widened.

"Try it."

She stopped adjacent to the gap in the parked cars. Her finger hesitated over the button. "Are you sure about this?"

"Yep." I pushed it for her, and the steering wheel began to turn by itself.

"I don't like this," screamed Emily. "Make it stop."

"Sit back and relax," I said, folding my hands in my lap as the car inched forwards and backwards. "Active Parking Assist. My ex-husband owned a car with this feature. Handy, when you're as bad a driver as I am. He bought it after I pranged his Rolls Royce for the third time."

"I can't sit back and relax," said Emily, her hands poised an inch away from the wheel. "It's taking all my self-control not to grab it. This is plain witchery."

"There," I said, as the electric car finished demonstrating its abilities and rested neatly in a parking space marginally longer than itself. "That wasn't too hard, was it?"

"I'm still shaking," said Emily. "I want my Morris Minor back. At least I can trust that not to pootle off without me."

We stepped out of the car and stood on the pavement. Grey clouds scudded across a sky that threatened rain, and a stiff breeze blew litter down the street.

I held the phone up again and compared the view on its screen with the streetscape in front of me. "We're probably standing exactly where the photographer was when he took this picture," I said.

Emily glanced at the phone, then up at the factory chimney. "Okay. I admit it. You're right. This must be the same place. But how does this help us?"

"I'm glad you're saying 'us', Emily. Because I can't do this on my own." I squeezed her hand, and she smiled.

"I'm sorry I got grumpy with you," she said. "You're right; we should try to prove it was Mary's skeleton in the car and bring closure for her family. Closure for the poor woman's brother, who only has a few weeks to live."

"Are you two lost?" A short, middle-aged woman with a strong, local accent accosted us. "You're not from around here; I can tell that from your posh clothes. You're standing in Brickworks Terrace, if that helps."

"We're not lost. But could you confirm if we're in the right place? We're looking for the spot where this photo was taken." I showed her my phone.

She inspected the screen over her glasses, dropped her umbrella, clutched her chest and slumped against me.

CHAPTER TWENTY-TWO

"Quick, Emily, help me. I can't support her." We eased the woman into a sitting position on the pavement, where she regained consciousness and blinked.

"Are you okay?" I handed her the umbrella. "What happened?"

"Hmph. A funny turn. I have them sometimes. Lift me up, would you?"

"Would you like us to call an ambulance?" asked Emily.

"What good will an ambulance do?" said the woman. "I'm not ill. What I need is a nice, strong cup of tea."

"Do you live near here?" I asked. "Could we make sure you reach home safely?"

"Number thirty-two." She pointed with her umbrella. "Blue door."

Emily and I helped her up and held onto her arms as she wobbled towards her house in the middle of the terrace.

"I've no idea what came over me," she muttered. "Soon be right with a nice pot of tea. Will you two be having one?"

"Thank you," I said. "We need to make sure you're all right before we leave you alone."

Plus, we need to discover why you collapsed as soon as you saw that picture.

The lady tugged a bunch of keys from a pocket and unlocked the front door, which led directly into a small living room. Two easy chairs stood at right angles to each other covered in beige fabric. They were angled towards a brown, art déco-style fire in the centre of one wall, and an ancient television teetered on spindly legs in the corner. A sash window with a small dining table and two wooden chairs in front of it gave a view onto the street.

"Do you live alone?" asked Emily. "Is there anyone we could call?"

"No one that would care," she said. "And yes, I've lived by myself the last twenty years, since my mother died. Not even a cat to keep me company. Mother was allergic to cats, so we never had one."

"D'you want to sit down, and I'll make the tea?" asked Emily. "You've had a shock."

"I'll not be having any guests of mine make their own tea, thank you very much. So what do they call you two?"

Emily and I glanced at each other. "What does who call us?" I asked.

"People. What are your names? I'm Nora."

"Oh. I'm Shiraz, and this is Emily."

"Don't stand there like muppets, then. Take your coats off and make yourselves at home while I brew the tea."

Suitably admonished, we sat.

"What on earth happened outside?" whispered Emily.

"Nora saw the photo on my phone and passed out."

"I wonder why she'd do that?"

"I'm afraid to ask in case she faints again. Or worse. D'you think we should call an ambulance?"

"She was quite insistent we shouldn't. She seems very independent."

"Stubborn, more like."

Nora returned with a tray containing a white teapot, a milk jug, three cups and a plate with three Bourbon biscuits on it. For some reason, they were considerably smaller than I remembered from my childhood teatime treat.

"One of us must be in your usual seat," said Emily.

"Indeed you are. No matter. I'll pull up another." She lifted one of the dining chairs and dragged it forward. "I don't know what came over me. One minute I was giving you two directions to somewhere, the next I'm on the pavement. Good job I didn't break anything." She sat and began to pour tea.

"Definitely," I said, wondering how I could steer the conversation back to the photo. "Have you lived here long, Nora?"

"Young lass, I was born in this house. My parents brought up six children here. And I'm the only one who never left home." She laughed. "The only home I've ever had."

I glanced through to the kitchen, then at the steep staircase and wondered how a family of two adults and six children could have lived in such a small dwelling.

"You'd know all the families in the street, then?" I asked.

"Not these days." Nora shook her head. "Maybe I did years ago. Too many people from other places have come here now. When I was young, everybody knew their neighbours, and we all trusted each other. You could leave your front door unlocked without a worry. Not like now. The place has changed. In those days, all the men worked in the factory, and some of the women too. Modern machinery and foreign imports have put an end to that. Not so much work for people here now."

"Did you work in the factory, Nora?"

"Did I heck. There's no way I would've stood on a production line all day. No, indeed. I had myself a job at the supermarket in town. Better conditions, better money and better hours."

She paused and sipped tea. I decided to risk her having another funny turn.

"Nora, out on the street, I showed you a photo."

"You didn't. I never saw no photo."

"On my phone. Here." I unlocked my iPhone and displayed Bill Leonard's copy of the newspaper article, which he'd taken in the Hebblethwaite's house forty-seven years previously.

Nora peered over her glasses and shook her head slowly. "Well I never. I suppose that's why I came over all wobbly. I didn't think I'd ever see that devil again." She held the phone and stared at it. "Wherever did you get this picture?" She turned the phone over in her hand like someone would a printed photograph, to see if anything was written on the back.

"The photo's from a newspaper cutting. It was taken outside your house, wasn't it? D'you know the people in it?"

"Aye. I know them all right." She sat back and folded her arms.

"Who are they, Nora? How d'you know them?"

"The one on the end's me."

"You?" My gaze shifted between the phone and her, then I showed the picture again to Emily, who shrugged.

"A much younger me, granted," continued Nora, "but that's me all right. The bride was my bestest friend, Mary. We worked together at the supermarket, and I was her bridesmaid. Of course, I was surprised when she suddenly decided to marry him"—she spat the word and jabbed her finger at the phone— "but with her parents passing away, and her being forced to look after the boy, I understood why she needed the financial security."

"Who was her husband, Nora, and why did you call him a devil?"

"His name was Patrick. I can't remember how or where they met, but I do recall her rushing into work one morning as I was putting on my uniform in the staff room. She seemed out of breath and excited. I knew she'd had a terrible time recently, with her little brother being caught for stealing. Poor girl; no way could she bring him up as if she was his mother and father rolled into one. She was only eighteen, I think, when their parents died. So when she came into work all happy and grinning, I reckoned it was the first time I'd seen her smile in months."

Nora paused and poured a second cup of tea. "So I asked her, 'What are you looking so cheery about?' and she replied she'd met a man and the best thing was, he had a job and even a sports car. I looked at her suspiciously, because she'd never been courting to my knowledge, and I asked when she was going to introduce us. Then she told me he was picking her up from work and taking her to meet his parents to talk about marriage. I was astounded. She'd gone from being a teenage single parent of her younger brother to just about a married woman in less than a week. Anyway, knock-off time came, and she skipped out of the staff entrance where we found this man waiting, standing next to a blue, two-seater, open-topped car. Mary introduced us, but I didn't like him. Something wasn't right about his manner. I have a sixth sense for people, and this chap gave me the willies."

"What was wrong with him, Nora?" I asked. "What didn't you like?"

"I couldn't put my finger on it immediately, but after Mary had climbed into the passenger seat, I leant over the car to say goodbye to her. Then, I noticed it. I noticed what was wrong with him. My mother always used to say to me, 'Never trust a man whose eyes aren't the same colour. They're the devil's apprentices.' And this chap looked up at me, and I could see he had one green eye, and one blue. That's what was wrong with him. He was a servant of Lucifer." She sat back and nodded emphatically. "The devil. And that's what he turned out to be. Him and that other bloke in the suit."

"Why, Nora? What happened? They seem happy in the wedding photo."

"Mary turned up to work the following day, and explained the meeting with his parents didn't go well. I couldn't understand what the problem was exactly, but then she said they were getting married that Friday, and would I like to be her bridesmaid? Naturally, my first thought was that she'd got herself into trouble; that was the usual reason for quick weddings in those days, but she'd only known him a week or two, so that wasn't possible."

"Got herself into trouble?" asked Emily.

"With child, young lass, with child."

"Oh." Emily blushed, and Nora continued.

"Anyway, Friday came, and she'd borrowed some kind of white affair, and he'd put on a suit, and I wore my best dress, which didn't match her frock, but never mind. I thought we'd be going to St Michael's Church, but this man of hers turned up in a taxi and took us, together with Mary's younger brother, around to a room by the council offices. An official made a little speech, pronounced them man and wife and asked me to sign a piece of paper to say I was a witness.

"What about the fourth person in the photo? The best man, I presume?"

"I'd never met him," said Nora. "He was a friend of the groom and joined us at the wedding place. D'you know, once we left there, he nipped back to our street, covered the little blue sports car in balloons and painted 'Just Married' on it in some kind of spray. I don't think Patrick was too impressed with that."

"So why did Patrick turn out to be a devil?" prompted Emily.

"Because he took my best friend Mary away from me and away from her brother. He took her someplace, and I never saw her again. I've always wondered what happened to her. Her brother disappeared shortly after, too. New people moved into their house, and that was the end of that. Until you two turn up and show me that picture. No wonder I fainted."

Nora frowned and turned to me. "You're not detectives, are you? D'you know where Mary is, after all these years?"

"We're not detectives," I said. "But I think we know where Mary is."

"You do?" Nora's eyes lit up, and I could almost see the years fall off her, back to being the teenage supermarket cashier with no more worries than which outfit to wear to the weekend dance.

She leant forward and grabbed my arm. "Could you tell me where she is? I'd give anything to see her again."

"I'm sorry, Nora." Emily's mouth formed a straight line. "We believe she's passed away."

I glared at her and whispered through clenched teeth, "We're not supposed to say that."

"Passed away?" asked Nora. "I suppose she must've been sixty-five; same age as me. Was she ill?"

Too late now.

"Um, we think she may've died not long after you last saw her."

"What? How? She was only eighteen."

"She may've been killed in an accident. We don't have any details. That's what we're trying to discover. That's why we asked you if this was the street in the photo."

"An accident? What kind of accident? Did he kill her? I wouldn't be surprised."

She paused, as if she wasn't sure whether to tell us something.

"Her husband returned here, y'know. Back to Milltown. I saw him."

CHAPTER TWENTY-THREE

I gasped at Nora's revelation. "Did I hear you correctly? Mary's husband? He came back here? Are you sure it was him?"

"Yep. He'd dyed his hair and grown a beard, but he couldn't fool me. I served him in the supermarket."

"Sorry to doubt you, Nora; how could you be certain it was Patrick?"

"A man can change his appearance, but he can't change his eye colour. And I looked straight at him over the cash register, and I said, 'So you're back. Is Mary with you?' He pretended not to know what I meant, and claimed I'd mistaken him for someone else. But I knew I hadn't. There was a queue for the till, so I couldn't stop him from leaving. But I know who I saw." She sat back and folded her arms. "The devil in human form."

"Nora." I leant forward. "This is important. How long after the wedding did you serve Patrick in Milltown supermarket?"

"Maybe a month? Six weeks?"

"And did you see him after that?"

"Never. And I never saw Mary, either. I reported it to the police. I told them he'd done something to her. They didn't take me seriously; me, a teenage shop assistant. They told me I was mistaken. But I wasn't. And what you've told me confirms it. After all these years. Poor, poor girl."

Nora's story troubled me as Emily drove us back to our accommodation. We'd discovered the spot where the wedding photo had been taken quite by accident and, through fortune, we'd found a witness to the wedding who was able to fill in many of the gaps. But her account raised more questions than answers.

Who was this mysterious best man?

Why did Patrick Hebblethwaite return alone to Milltown?

And why did he deny his identity when Nora recognised him?

Emily parked the car outside the bed-and-breakfast. On a recommendation from our host, we visited a local gastropub which served food on Sunday evenings. The waitress sat us at a table for two near the window from where we could watch the streetlamps illuminate, and night gradually fall. Each place setting comprised two knives, two forks, a spoon and a side plate containing a small bread roll. We ordered a bottle of wine and studied the menu.

"Why don't you open the Wicked Whelk for dinner, Emily?" I asked, spreading butter on my bread. "I reckon you'd do well."

Emily gave me a withering look. "I get up at five. I open the café at six, and I'm flat out making teas, coffees and toasted sandwiches and serving cakes and filled rolls until two. If I'm lucky, there's a lull mid-morning when I can take a breather. Then, after closing, I clean up, prepare for the next day and if needed, zip off to the wholesaler. You should try it. This is actually a nice holiday for me." She tapped her roll on the table and prised it apart. "These aren't fresh. They were made yesterday. Or frozen. Cheats. I'd never do that. And they've got three staff on. Easy life."

"You know I'll help you in the café."

Emily reached over and held my arm. "Shiraz, I appreciate the offer; I really do. But, um, it's obvious you haven't worked in hospitality before."

"Is that a nice way of saying I'm hopeless in the kitchen?"

She blushed. "You're not hopeless. But some of us have skills that others don't. If you know what I mean. You're good at, um..."

She looked at me, and we both laughed.

"I'm good at getting us into mischief?"

"Yep, you can say that again. What on earth are we up to our necks in this time?"

"Here's what I think," I said, lowering my voice and leaning towards her. "We know Patrick and Mary eloped. Bill Leonard discovered that fact when he visited Patrick's parents and spoke with his mother. They ran off to Milltown, where Mary lived. For whatever reason, they were married immediately at the Milltown registry office with three people present. Nora, who was the bridesmaid, another man who was a friend of Patrick's, and Mary's younger brother, John."

"And obviously there was someone performing the ceremony as well." The wine arrived, and Emily poured a glass for both of us.

"Right. Six people were at the ceremony, including the bride and groom. Then they returned to Nora's house, maybe for an after-wedding tea, they discovered Patrick's car had been decorated by the best man, and a photographer from the local paper snapped them, which is the picture I have on my phone."

"I wonder why he did that?"

"The Milltown newspaper probably published a photo of every local wedding. Gosh, when I married Monty, three newspapers and *Red Carpet Superstars* magazine all sent their paparazzi. Anyway, Patrick and Mary were married. At that point, according to John Smith's account, Patrick slipped him fifty pounds, more money than he'd ever seen, told him he's taking his sister away, and said they'll send for him soon."

"Don't you think that's a little odd?" asked Emily.

"What, Patrick giving John fifty pounds?"

"No, Mary abandoning her brother. He was only seventeen, wasn't he?"

"As far as she was aware, they were going to send for young John in a few days, as soon as they were settled wherever they were going. And I suppose Patrick's car only had two seats, so maybe the plan was for Patrick to return by himself and collect him. But I think"—I tapped the side of my nose—"Patrick Hebblethwaite had no such intentions."

"Ooh. Have you worked out what he was up to?"

"We have jigsaw pieces, Emily. Some of them are missing."

"Yes. And we don't have the picture of the cat on the box to help us."

"The cat?"

"All my jigsaws are of cats."

"Got it. And," I said, patting both hands on the table top, "some of the pieces are still upside down. I think we've taken the jigsaw analogy as far as it will go. For whatever reason, Patrick brought Mary to Redcliff-upon-Sea, specifically Golden Beach."

"That's one of the upside down pieces," said Emily. "Why Golden Beach? What connection did he have with a seaside village all the way down there?"

"Who knows? Anyway, within a few weeks of them arriving, the landslip and the destruction of Golden Beach occurred on Valentine's night. And poor eighteen-year-old newly married Mary gets poisoned, bundled into a car and shoved over the edge of a cliff to make it look like she'd died in the disaster."

"If Oscar were here," said Emily, "he'd tell you your theory's on shaky ground."

"He's not here, so I can theorise all I like. Humour me. Let's say that's exactly how it happened. Next, having done the deed, Patrick Hebblethwaite makes his way north, back to Milltown. He's altered his appearance somewhat, growing a beard and changing his hair colour. That could've all happened while he was living in the South with Mary. But what he can't change is the colour of his eyes. And six weeks after the wedding, Nora sees him in the supermarket and recognises him. She demands to know what Patrick's done with her best friend, and Patrick pretends she's mistaken him for someone else. Don't you think that's suspicious?"

"Maybe it was someone else with the same eyes?"

"How many people d'you know with eyes of different colours?"

"None."

"Right. Me neither. I think she saw Patrick."

Emily drained her glass. "This jigsaw's very incomplete, isn't it?"

"Yep. We need to find more of the pieces and turn them the right way up."

She yawned. "I hope they take our food order soon. I'm looking forward to a yummy dinner, then having an early night. The train leaves for Redcliff at 9:00 tomorrow morning."

"Ah, yes. About that. Um, would you mind returning to Redcliff by yourself?"

Emily frowned. "You're not coming with me?"

"You're welcome to hang around too, but you need to open the café on Tuesday, don't you?"

"Of course. But why are you staying?"

"Because one of us needs to turn over more puzzle pieces. I'll return to Redcliff in a day or two. I want to visit Nora again. There's one guest at the wedding we haven't tracked down."

"The best man? Nora didn't know him."

"She might remember something which shows us more of the picture on the box."

Emily and I drove to the railway station together the following morning. The streets were public-holiday quiet, and traffic was light.

"Thanks for coming with me," I said, after we'd handed the dreaded electric car back to the rental company, and we waited on the station platform. "I wish you could stay too. It's a shame you can't call in sick."

"Shiraz, I own the café. Who would I call? Myself? 'Hello Emily, it's Emily. Emily can't come to work today because Emily's busy on one of her friend Shiraz's wild duck chases'."

"Goose chases."

"Whatever."

The approaching train's whistle sounded.

"I'm probably going to regret this," said Emily, "but is there anything I could do to help while you're tracking down the best man?"

"Could you visit John Smith in the hospital? Find out how he is, and see if we can get him reunited with his dog? He'll be missing him terribly, and I'm sure Oscar'll be sick of Rebel and Cadbury tearing around his garden on their rampage of destruction."

"All right. I'll drop in tomorrow, after closing. When d'you think you'll return?"

"If not tomorrow, then Wednesday." I winked. "It depends how many jigsaw pieces I find and whether I can complete the cat picture."

Emily boarded the train, and we hugged through the carriage door's open window.

"Bye, Shiraz. Be careful. Look after yourself. Don't get kidnapped or anything."

"I promise I won't. I'll see you very soon."

The train pulled away, and I watched its rear red lights until they disappeared around a bend. I shivered. Suddenly, Milltown felt lonely and unsafe.

A silver taxi dropped me back in Nora's street.

"Here you are, Love," said the taxi driver. "Thirty-two, Brickworks Terrace. Though I can't see what a smartly dressed lady like you would be doing in these parts."

"Visiting an old friend," I said. "How much do I owe you?"

I paid him and stepped out. The vista was identical to the previous day. The same red-brick, terraced houses, the same grey pavement, the same factory chimney at the end of the street.

Eerie. Unchanged and unchanging.

Number thirty-two's blue door was ajar. I remembered Nora's statement about how she left it open in the old days, and wondered if she still did sometimes. I knocked and stood back.

No answer.

I rapped louder and called, "Hello? Nora?"

Nothing.

I poked my head inside. "Nora? It's Shiraz, from yesterday. Hello?"

As I pushed the door open, I found Nora lying motionless on the floor.

CHAPTER TWENTY-FOUR

"Nora!" I shouted, as my marine rescue first aid training kicked in.

D—check for danger. Where to start?

R—Response. "Nora, can you hear me? Open your eyes. What's your name? Squeeze my hands." I shouted all these in the right order, surprising myself at how well I'd remembered them in a real-life situation. But Nora didn't move.

S—Send for help. I plucked my phone from my pocket and dialled the emergency number. My fingers trembled, and I struggled to press the three digits.

"Emergency. Which service, please?"

"Ambulance."

"Hold on, caller." A pause, then a second dial tone, followed by another voice. I glanced at Nora's face, which was a horrid alabaster colour.

"Milltown Ambulance."

"Emergency operator connecting you with mobile 07700 900119."

"Your reference MAS78934. Go ahead, caller."

"Help! I'm with an elderly woman who's collapsed."

"What's your name?"

"Shiraz."

"What address are you at?"

"Thirty-two, um, Brickworks Road."

"Brickworks Terrace, Milltown?"

"Yes.

"Is she breathing?"

"No. I'm first aid trained."

"Have you checked her airways?"

"No. Hang on. Okay, they're clear."

"Have you checked for a response?"

"Yes. Nothing."

"Do you know how to give CPR?"

"Yes. But I've never done it for real."

"Commence CPR immediately. Put your phone on speaker where you can hear me. The ambulance is on its way. Thirty compressions. Hands in the centre of the chest below the breastbone. Ready? One. Two. Three..."

The paramedic on the end of the phone talked me through the thirty chest pumps in a rhythmic, practiced voice.

"Put your cheek above her mouth. Can you feel her exhale?"

"No. She's not breathing."

"Deliver two rescue breaths."

Nora's skin felt cold and clammy. "I'm sorry, I don't think I can do the breaths."

"Continue with the compressions. One. Two. Three…"

I hadn't realised, while practising on a plastic dummy under Murph's supervision, how exhausting it was to give CPR. Two sets of thirty compressions, and my arms felt like I'd spent an hour on the push-up machine at the gym. My chest pumping continued robotically as the voice speaking from my phone counted over and over.

A distant siren sounded.

"Maintain the rhythm until the ambulance staff relieve you. Any change in the patient?"

"She's still not breathing." I carried on pushing Nora's chest, as the siren wailed to a stop outside, and two paramedics bashed the door open. "Shiraz?" said one.

I looked up at her in the middle of compressions and nodded. "Twenty-eight, Twenty-nine. Thirty." I took my hands off Nora's chest.

"Can you keep going?" asked the paramedic.

I shook my head and slumped back.

"How many sets of compressions have you completed?" she asked, as she knelt and began pumping.

"Loads." I panted and scraped my hands through my hair.

"Eighteen," said the voice on the speaker.

The other paramedic felt Nora's neck and shone a torch into her eyes.

The paramedics conversed using words I didn't understand. 'Hypostasis' and 'Livor Mortis'.

"I'm sorry, Miss," said the second one, finally. "You've been amazing. But she's probably been dead for hours."

I collapsed against the same chair I'd sat in while talking with Nora only the day before. What was happening in my life? This kind of event wasn't in the plan when I decided to become a marine rescue volunteer. My arms and shoulders ached, and I rubbed them.

A second siren wailed outside, followed by car doors slamming, and heavy boots marching across the pavement. Two police officers entered: a young, slim woman and a plump, red-faced, middle-aged man sporting a walrus moustache.

"Constable Keith Lumley from Milltown police," said the man. "This is Constable Gemma Dinsdale." The young officer nodded at me, glanced at Nora's body and visibly whitened. I guessed she hadn't seen a corpse before. Neither had I, except a very decomposed one.

"What have we here, Debbie?" Constable Keith asked the senior paramedic.

"Morning, Keith. Female, aged around sixty, found by this lady,"—she indicated me—"who performed CPR at the scene but was unable to resuscitate."

Constable Keith gave me a look of commiseration. "Well done, Miss. You did your best." He turned to the paramedic. "Cause of death?"

She frowned. "Keith, you know I'm not permitted or qualified to tell you that."

"Come on, Debbie, we're old friends," said Constable Keith. "At least give me an educated guess."

"Keith Lumley, you'll get me fired, you will. All right. If I was a betting woman, and I'm not, I'd say she could've been strangled. There's bruising commensurate with the neck being restricted.

"Strangled?" asked Constable Gemma. "Are you intimating she was murdered? It wasn't a heart attack?"

"It's hard to strangle yourself," said the paramedic. "Have you tried it? No, don't. I've enough to deal with one death. I've said enough. Wait for pathology."

Their gallows humour surprised me, but I kept quiet.

"This is a now a crime scene," said Constable Keith. "Could everybody please remain here until released?"

Constable Gemma rubbed my upper arm. "You poor thing. You tried so hard to revive her. Did you know the deceased? Were you a friend, or relative?"

"I met her for the first time yesterday. I'm researching, um, family history, and I came to this street trying to find more information about this photograph." I picked up my phone from where it had broadcasted the paramedic's CPR instructions through its speaker and showed them the wedding picture. "While I was checking I was at the same place where the photo was taken, this woman approached me and asked if I needed directions. Then, for some reason, she had a medical episode, and I helped her inside her house, where we had a chat over tea."

Constable Keith frowned. "And now, the following day, she's turned up dead, and you, who only met her yesterday, happen to be the one to find her?"

"What are you inferring? If I had anything to do with her death, why would I have exhausted myself performing CPR?"

"Sorry, Miss, I'll still need you to help us with our inquiries." He turned to his younger colleague. "Get on the blower to Detective Creaser."

"This is becoming a habit," I muttered.

"Pardon, Miss?"

"Nothing, Officer."

CHAPTER TWENTY-FIVE

Monday, 5th April 1976

"You. What are you doing here?" The figure lying on the filthy, discarded mattress sat up to find a bearded man standing over him. "How did you find me? Is Mary with you?"

"She's coming, John." The man with the beard spoke in a low, calm voice. "We'll all be together shortly. One happy family."

"It's cold at night, sleeping in this empty factory. I miss home. I miss Mary. I'm hungry."

"You'll see Mary very soon." A bank note passed between them. "Here. Buy yourself some groceries. And warm clothes." The bearded man crouched and glanced over his shoulder. No one could overhear their conversation but, even so, he lowered his voice. "When Mary and I return for good, we'll all live together in the countryside. You'll have your own bedroom and your own comfy bed."

"Are you coming back now?"

"Soon, John. To my house in the country. But you can stay there tonight. Would you like that?"

"What d'you think? Of course I would." The figure on the mattress swept his arm around the dingy storage area, where scuttling rats kept him awake. "When will Mary arrive?"

"Before long. In a few days, I'll bring her with me, and we'll all live together. But, first, you have to help me. Some people might come looking for me, John. I need you to use your brains; use your cunning. Divert them by whatever means you can think of."

"Why are they looking for you?"

"I can't tell you that. They're bad people, and they'll want to take me away. If you tell them you've seen me, you'll never be with Mary again. I'm in danger but, with your help, it'll pass."

The figure lying on the mattress swallowed hard and nodded.

The bearded man stood. "I'll always look after you. You know that. We're family. Now, get up. Come with me. I'll buy you breakfast. Tell me everything. I want to hear your story; get to know you better. And then I'll show you where you're going to live. It's time to start your new life."

"With Mary and you?"

"All in good time, John. Patience."

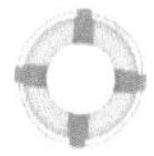

CHAPTER TWENTY-SIX

Detective Inspector Michael Creaser clumped up Nora's steps and introduced himself. The two constables earwigged as I explained who I was, and what I was doing in Milltown. I didn't hide anything, telling the detective every detail about the landslip, the Triumph Spitfire, Mary and John Smith; even Rebel the dog got a mention. I finished by explaining again how I came to be there.

"That's some story," said Inspector Creaser. "I wonder how it ties in with Nora's death? Who would have any reason to strangle her?"

"I've no idea," I said, hoping he'd see me as an ally, a colleague even, rather than a suspect. "Of course, it may be nothing to do with it. She might've surprised a burglar when she came home or had some other enemy we know nothing about."

He closed his notebook. "You may be right, Miss. But I don't like coincidences."

I recalled Oscar saying exactly the same, and wondered if it was standard police training.

"Do you have anything else to tell me?" he asked.

"No, but I don't suppose you'd be able to look up Patrick Hebblethwaite for me on the police computer?"

"Of course not," Constable Keith interjected. "We can't research people like a phone directory and give out information to members of the public."

"He's right," said Inspector Creaser. "But what are you trying to find out?"

"There's a chance he might be connected with Nora's death."

He tilted his head. "What, exactly, are you inferring?"

"You've heard my story. You know, over forty years ago, Patrick Hebblethwaite returned here, leaving behind a dead young wife in a car. Nora told me she saw him, and he refused to admit who he was. Can we at least look him up and see if he has a police record?"

"We can. But be aware, we've no reason to tell you if he has."

"You don't have to tell me anything. I'm quietly suggesting you inspect your records. Investigate Patrick Hebblethwaite. In connection with this live murder case. You don't like coincidences, remember?"

I lay on the bed at my accommodation. The empty single mattress on the opposite side of the room betrayed Emily's absence, and I missed her company, her funny laugh, her way of suddenly coming up with new, unlikely theories and declaring our investigation over by saying, 'Case closed'. I realised she was the best friend I'd ever had. Certainly since my school days. Probably my primary school days. All the girls at Thornhill Grange Ladies' College spoke about people behind their backs. I'd probably done that too. Still, I went on to become a model and the wife of a rich society man. Which meant absolutely nothing, did it? Nothing. That pointless, vapid existence I'd lived. I thumped the mattress. And what was I doing now? I was alone, in a strange town, trying to unearth what happened to a girl I had nothing to do with, and all for the sake of my own stupid curiosity.

The phone ringing disturbed my train of thought, and I grinned when I saw Emily's name on it. "Hi," I said. "Where are you?"

"Crewe. I've changed trains. This journey takes forever. What's the news?"

"Nora's dead."

"Nora from yesterday?"

"Yes."

"What? But she seemed fine, apart from her funny turn."

"Someone strangled her. I discovered her and tried to perform CPR, but it was too late."

"Woah. Are you okay? What a horrible experience. Poor woman. Who would do that?"

"No idea. I'm coming home; I'm sick of all this."

"Good idea, Shiraz. Give up all this investigating. These deaths are taking a toll on your mental health."

"See you tomorrow. I miss you."

I began to pack my clothes, ready to catch the next train back to Redcliff, then stopped myself. What about John Smith? Wouldn't he want me to tie up the ends of this story? He was probably still in Redcliff Hospital, missing his dog, missing his sister, ruminating on his life and wondering how things could've been different if Patrick Hebblethwaite had never taken her away from him. I unpacked my clothes again and sat on the edge of the bed with my head in my hands.

What now? What do I do?

My mobile rang again, and I grabbed it.

"Shiraz Jones?"

"Yes?"

"Constable Gemma Dinsdale from Milltown Police." Her voice was low, as if she didn't want to be overheard.

"Hi. How can I help?"

"I looked up your Patrick Hebblethwaite."

I sat bolt upright. "And?"

"I shouldn't tell you this, but it's public knowledge if you dig deep enough. He did have a police record."

"For murder?"

"No. There was only one entry on his sheet, and it wasn't murder." Her voice dropped to a whisper. "In 1976, while resisting arrest at his farm in Hebble Bridge, Patrick

Hebblethwaite used an unlicensed shotgun to kill himself. He blew his head off."

The police constable began to speak louder, as if someone had come into the room. "Thank you, Miss, for your information. I'm sure we'll need to interview you again at some point. Goodbye for now."

"Wait," I said. "Stop. Before you go. Is there a newspaper here which might've reported his suicide?"

"Yes, I believe that would be the case," said Constable Gemma, enunciating her words clearly for the benefit of whoever was with her.

"Are their archives kept at the library?"

"Yes, that would be correct."

"Does it say in your records which month in 1976 he killed himself?"

"Very well. We *May* be in touch further."

Clever.

"Thank you, Officer Gemma. You've been very helpful. Goodbye."

"Goodbye, Ms Jones. And good luck."

I pressed 'end' on my phone and stared at the screen. Patrick Hebblethwaite had most likely murdered his young bride, returned to the Milltown area, changed his appearance and then killed himself. This didn't add up. And nothing intimated why he'd done any of that, so all I could do was guess. I opened a notepad on my phone and typed some ideas.

Theory one: Patrick wanted to marry Mary, but didn't want her younger brother in tow, so he made her abandon the boy with an empty promise they'd send for him later. When Mary realised that wasn't Patrick's intention, she threatened to leave him, and he killed her in Golden Beach and then came home to escape the crime.

Not bad, Shiraz, not bad.

Theory two: Mary didn't love Patrick, she only wanted him for the financial security; maybe she had a secret lover. Patrick discovered the affair and poisoned her, then put her in the car on the night of the landslide to make her death look like an accident.

Possible. But who was the secret lover? The best man, maybe?

Theory three:

The paper stayed blank. I couldn't think of a theory three. I wished Emily and Oscar were with me to brainstorm. And none of my ideas explained his suicide. A visit to the library was called for.

Unlike at Headland Bay, the Milltown library had computerised all their archives. I scrolled with the mouse and worked my way through May 1976. Stories about roadworks, upcoming summer events and a scandal of misappropriated funds at the local council gave way to a large headline and a photo.

The title read 'Suspect dies during arrest'. Underneath was a black-and-white image of three police cars outside a detached, stone cottage surrounded by low hills. I read the accompanying text.

'Patrick Hebblethwaite of Hebble Bridge near Milltown died yesterday at his home. Police knocked at the door of the remote family farmhouse, following up inquiries. While attempting to enter the property, a shot was heard. Police broke the door down and discovered Mr Hebblethwaite deceased with a shotgun in his hand. Mr Hebblethwaite, a hospital porter by trade, had recently returned from a short stay in the South and was believed to be separated from his wife.'

Believed to be separated from his wife? Bill Leonard would've had something to say about the quality of reporting. She was dead.

The article continued with an interview with a police inspector, who repeated everything it had described in his own words.

So the police had listened to Nora and had investigated Patrick Hebblethwaite. But following his suicide, they'd come up against a dead end, and with Mary buried in the landslide two hundred miles away in Redcliff-upon-Sea, and no national database of missing persons in those days, the investigation had become a cold case.

Until the new landslide uncovered the car, and Rebel the dog led me back to it.

My phone rang, displaying Emily's name.

"Hiya," I answered it quietly. "I'm in a library. Did you reach home okay?"

"Five hours on two trains with no one to talk to. Luckily, I had a good book."

"How are things in Redcliff?"

"Okay, thanks. Boots attacked me because I hadn't left him enough food. Oh, and there's something you should know. I went to see John Smith as you asked, but he wasn't in hospital anymore."

"Had he recovered?"

"Not officially. He discharged himself on Sunday."

"That's odd. He must've been missing Rebel."

"But he hasn't collected Rebel. Oscar still has him. And John doesn't know where Oscar lives."

"Great. He's gone missing. I can't worry about that now. I've got bigger fish to fry here in Milltown. Patrick Hebblethwaite committed suicide at Hebble Bridge in May 1976, the same year as the landslip."

"Wow. Nora was right; she did see him. Hang on, was that after Bill Leonard went north and met his parents?"

"Yes, and immediately following their meeting, the parents passed away." I paused and rubbed my chin. "Emily, do we have a serial killer on our hands? That's five deaths."

"Five?"

"Mary, Patrick Hebblethwaite's parents, Patrick himself and Nora."

"But Patrick killed himself. And Nora's death was forty-seven years later. They can't be connected."

"I don't like coincidences."

Gosh. I'm beginning to talk like a police officer.

"Come home, Shiraz," said Emily. "Please. You're out of your depth."

"I will. Tomorrow. On the early train. I must find John and tell him I haven't been able to discover what happened to his sister. He doesn't even know she's dead yet, for goodness' sake."

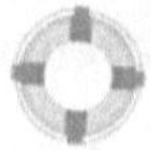

I stood on Milltown station platform with my Louis Vuitton overnight bag in my hand. A takeaway double shot skinny latte warmed my other palm, but it wasn't as tasty as Emily's coffee.

"Good morning, Ladies and Gentlemen. The next train on platform two will be the 9:17 for Crewe, where passengers should change for all lines to the South. Please stand back from the platform as the train approaches."

I gazed up the empty track, searching for the oncoming train. My trip to the North had been a complete failure. I'd hoped to discover more about the mystery of Mary's death, but all I'd found was confusion and dead ends. The only murder which was being investigated was Nora's, and I'd allow the police to handle that one. She was a nice enough person and didn't deserve to die, but I didn't know her from a bar of soap. My hands shook as I recalled performing CPR on her without success.

The train came to a stop, and I opened the door to a carriage. As it slammed behind me, my phone rang.

"Ms Jones? Detective Inspector Michael Creaser from Milltown police."

"Hello, Officer. I'm just boarding a train at Milltown station, and I'm going home. So if you want to question me further about Nora's murder, we'll have to do it over the phone."

"I don't want to ask you about Nora's murder. We've arrested a suspect; I thought you'd like to know."

"Great. Thank you for telling me. I hope justice is done."

"Ms Jones, he's not only confessed to Nora's killing. He knows something about the historic case you mentioned. The body in the landslip."

The train lurched and began to move slowly away from the platform.

"He does?"

"The girl in the car. The skeleton you were telling me about."

"Mary Hebblethwaite? Did he say it was Mary Hebblethwaite?"

Slow clackety-clacks sounded, as the train gradually picked up speed.

"Yes, Mary Hebblethwaite," said Inspector Creaser. "He has information about her death."

"Keep him there. Don't let him go." I glanced out of the window as the station buildings glided past. "I'm coming to the police station. Right now."

I grabbed my bag, opened the train door and stared at the moving ground beneath me.

And jumped.

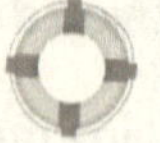

CHAPTER TWENTY-SEVEN

Patrick Hebblethwaite swivelled his head and studied his surroundings.

Was this the place where he needed to be?

His memories troubled him, gnawed at what little soul he had.

Memories of a time long ago, when life was different.

Simpler. Before all of... this.

There'd been many places, and this place, right here, was only one of them.

One solitary, lonely place.

Regardless, the time was now.

Time to live in the present. Not the future, or the past.

He was at the point of no return.

No going back.

The past would never exist again, and the future might not either.

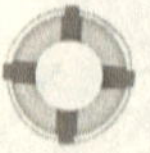

CHAPTER TWENTY-EIGHT

My crash landing on the ground hurt more than I expected, and I shrieked. The case flew from my hands as I tumbled across the grass and smashed into a blackberry bush. I opened my eyes gradually and assessed the pain. Each limb could still move, and my eyes could open, although the close-up foliage looked blurry.

"Madam! Madam."

A distant voice. A young voice, with an accent.

"Madam!" The voice became louder. "Are you okay? What happened?"

A man wearing a turban came into my field of vision, and I had a brief, random flashback to Karam the paramedic. My first thought was wondering when I'd see him again, which probably wasn't the most appropriate in my current situation.

"Madam," said the turban wearer. "You are alive. Praise to the Gods."

I pushed myself to my knees, shook my hair out, rubbed my eyes and stared at him. He wore a smart, light-blue jacket with a red logo.

"Are you a taxi driver?" I asked.

"Yes, but Madam, you need a hospital. Or a doctor. You fell from a moving train."

He helped me to my feet. Everything hurt, my hands were covered in scratches, and I knew I'd have a bruise on my back. To my annoyance, I'd torn my Salvatore Ferragamo coat.

"Madam. I have your luggage." The taxi driver held up my Louis Vuitton case, which now sported a scuff mark down one side and a broken handle. "You gave me such a fright. I had delivered a passenger to the train, and I was about to leave when I saw you fall. Please, let me drive you to the hospital. I will not charge for this."

I brushed my coat and stretched my arms above my head. My hand skimmed a pain point on my face, and I winced. "I don't need a hospital. But could you please take me to the police station?"

"The police station, Madam? You fell from a train. You must let me take you to the hospital."

"The police station. I'm fine. And I'm happy to pay you. We need to leave immediately."

The middle-aged, female desk sergeant looked up from the pad she wrote on. "Yes?"

"I'm here to see Detective Inspector Creaser." I realised I presented an interesting sight. The taxi driver's passenger mirror had revealed a graze down one side of my face and dried leaves through my hair. It could've been a lot worse. At least I hadn't broken anything. Apart from the handle of my bag. And freshly applied concealer worked wonders.

"Wait here, please," she said.

Almost immediately, a side door opened, and Inspector Creaser marched through. He looked me up and down. "What happened to you? Have you had an accident?"

"I fell over. Could I use your bathroom?"

"Certainly. And then we need to talk."

I stared in the rectangular, metal mirror in the police station's toilets. It didn't reflect as well as glass, and my face appeared blurry as if I was viewing it through a swimming pool. I dabbed the red welt down my left cheekbone with damp toilet tissue.

The detective waited outside the bathroom and showed me into a white-painted, brightly lit, utilitarian room with four chairs, two either side of a Formica-topped table. It resembled the examination room at Redcliff police station where Bert and Sergeant Will had interviewed Emily and me, and I wondered if police architects chose their station designs from a standard catalogue.

Inspector Creaser reviewed notes on his pad, while I waited.

He cleared his throat. "As I mentioned on the phone, we have a man in custody connected with the death of a female known to you, Nora Stubbins."

"She wasn't known to me. I told you yesterday; we'd only met once. I'd never heard her surname before you said it then. But congratulations. You arrested this man very quickly."

"Good, old-fashioned police work. We completed house to house enquiries, and a neighbour who habitually leaves his window open told us he'd heard two people arguing. English wasn't this man's first language, so we asked his teenage son to translate. Apparently, the man had been watching TV, when he heard raised voices from a neighbouring house; number thirty-two, Brickworks Terrace."

"That's Nora's house."

"Correct. This man had assumed there was some kind of domestic argument, so he ignored it. His son told us there were always arguments between people in Brickworks Terrace, although he'd never overheard the woman in number thirty-two shouting. A minute or two later, the man heard screaming, so he looked out of his window and saw a stocky, stooped figure wearing a grey coat leave Nora's house and jog up the street."

"Jog?"

"We think the meaning may've been lost in the translation. He remembered the figure had black hair, and a distinctive walk, with a limp. The person was trying to walk fast, trying to flee the scene, if you like, but they had something wrong with their leg."

"Is this the person you have in custody?"

"I'm coming to that. The shop further along Brickworks Terrace owns security cameras. We were able to watch footage of this stooped figure limping along the street and turning the corner. More security footage from a nearby factory then picked up the same person hobbling past their premises and disappearing down a neighbouring terrace. At that point, we lost him. But then we had a stroke of luck. I'd diverted a patrol car and, while they were talking to a group of teenagers on bikes who looked like they might be up to no good, a man fitting the description exited a house and stumbled away. The two officers gave chase, first in the car, then on foot, and apprehended him."

"Gosh. That was lucky."

The detective paused. "Criminals around here are normally young people, in their forties at the oldest. This man looked over seventy, which gave my two officers a shock."

"I'll bet it did."

"Anyway, they arrested him; we recorded his ID and fingerprints and looked him up on the police database. It turns out, the suspect we'd brought in was a career criminal. In his younger days, he'd been involved in armed robbery, grievous bodily harm and running a protection racket. He'd done time in prison for most of his life, although, as far as we could tell, he retired after his last stint, which was for attempted bank robbery."

"How long ago was that?"

He studied his notes. "He was released four years ago and seems to have kept his nose clean since."

"Until now."

"Correct. Until now. At the tender age of seventy-one, he committed his first murder."

"But what possible motive could he have for strangling Nora?"

"That's what we wondered. This was nothing like his former *modus operandi*, dealing with underworld figures, robbing banks, stealing cars, and so on. Nora Stubbins wasn't known to us and had no connection at all with the criminal scene. He confessed to killing her. He said he knew he'd be going to prison again, and he'd probably die there. But he claims it was manslaughter, not murder."

"Remind me of the difference?"

"Murder is where there's an intent to kill, to end life. A murderer means to kill their victim. Manslaughter's an accident. The killer might plan to injure their victim, not kill them. They die during the incident, but there's no intent."

"What have you charged him with?"

"We haven't, yet. During the interview, we attempted to find a motive. And it seems Nora and the suspect had a connection from decades ago. A tenuous connection, but a connection, nonetheless. And that's where you come in."

"Me?" I frowned and pointed at my chest.

"Yep. That photo you showed me."

"The one with the bride and groom in the street outside Nora's house?"

"That's the one. Four people in it. The bride, the groom, Nora the bridesmaid, and a fourth person."

"Do you mean...?"

"As they say at weddings, I do. It's time for the best man to make his speech."

CHAPTER TWENTY-NINE

I furrowed my brow at Inspector Creaser's statement.

Could this be Mary's murderer? The best man? What possible motive could he have? Was there something going on between him and the bride we know nothing about?

"Your story you related yesterday," said the detective. "The one about how this character Patrick Hebblethwaite married the girl Mary in the photo."

"Mary Smith, I believe, was her maiden name. I've met her brother, John."

"According to your account"—he referred to his notes—"Patrick and Mary married and moved away to a place called Golden Beach, where it seems Mary died during a natural disaster. Patrick may have returned here, so Nora told you. Patrick's parents passed away shortly afterwards, as reported by the priest you spoke with, and then Patrick killed himself while the police were trying to question him, which our records tell us. That's all we know about the events of 1976, and much of it's hearsay, because, you, Shiraz Jones, couldn't have known any of these people, as you weren't born then."

"Correct."

Inspector Creaser sighed and shuffled his papers.

"Let's move on to the present day. You find a body in a car, buried under a landslip, while engaged in your work as a marine rescue volunteer."

"Yes."

"You told us the car's number plate was J-O-Y 42. We've checked it, and that registration expired in January 1977. It was last registered to a Patrick Hebblethwaite." He looked up from his notes. "I think we can assume Patrick Hebblethwaite who owned J-O-Y 42 was the same Patrick Hebblethwaite in your photo."

I smiled. "I think we can."

"I've spoken with Redcliff police, and they told me the body was a female aged around twenty. The most logical conclusion is, it was Patrick's wife, Mary."

"Yes, that's what I believe."

"And you don't believe Mary's death was an accident because...?"

"Because the autopsy said she'd ingested a fatal dose of some medicine. Melar-something. Arsenic."

"How d'you know what's in the autopsy?"

"Um, a friend in the police told me. Also, it probably wasn't an accident, because she was in the passenger seat of the car. So she couldn't have driven the car over the edge. Someone pushed it over."

"Could she have been waiting for the driver at the time of the landslip? Maybe the car rolled over while he was trying to find the keys?"

"You said 'he'. I don't think you believe that theory for a minute."

Inspector Creaser smiled and raised one eyebrow. "You're sharp, Ms Jones. I'll give you that. So you conclude she was murdered, and for your own entertainment, you decide to investigate."

I crossed my arms. "It's not for my own entertainment. I'm trying to discover what became of Mary because I met her brother, John Smith. He doesn't have long to live, and I want him to know what happened to his sister before he passes away. At the moment, he doesn't even know she's dead."

"The local police may have told him."

"The local police might not yet be aware he's her brother."

The detective sighed again. "Then you turn up here, 250 miles north in Milltown. You show the photo of the wedding to a woman in the street, who, by complete coincidence, happens to be the bridesmaid in the picture." He clasped his hands in front of him and challenged me to respond.

"It wasn't a complete coincidence. We were standing in the exact spot the photo had been taken. She hadn't moved house since then."

"Okay. She invites you in, tells you about the wedding, tells you she didn't like the groom and says she never saw her friend Mary after that."

"Correct."

"Then, she mentions she set eyes on Patrick Hebblethwaite a few weeks later in the shop where she worked, but he'd changed his appearance, and he denied being who she thought he was."

"Also correct."

"Did she tell you anything else?"

"No. I was returning to ask her about the groom's best man when I found her dead."

"There are too many coincidences here, Ms Jones. Something else is going on, and I intend to put my finger on it."

"You mentioned the best man confessed to killing Nora?"

"He has. But we haven't discovered why, and I thought your history lesson from 1976 might help. But I can't see how it does."

"Have you asked him why?"

"Yes, but he hasn't been very forthcoming. We'll interview him again today."

"Could you let me know the outcome?"

"Why?" Inspector Creaser leant towards me across the table. "Who d'you think you are? Miss Marple? We'll let you know if we need more information from you."

"I'm trying to find closure for Mary's brother. That's all."

Streaks of rain crawled horizontally along the train windows. I curled myself into a foetal position across two seats in the near-empty carriage and stared at the drops, making silent bets with myself which one would reach the right-hand edge of the pane first. The view outside reflected my mood as the train passed a lonely farmhouse with one light on, illuminating the afternoon gloom for whoever was inside.

Lonely farmhouse.

Patrick Hebblethwaite.

All I had were a bunch of clues, none of which proved anything.

A murder. Or multiple murders.

Patrick Hebblethwaite killed his new wife. Why?

He then returned to his hometown. Why?

He disguised himself and denied he was who Nora recognised him to be when she served him in the supermarket. Why?

He may have murdered his parents. Why?

He then killed himself while resisting arrest. Why?

The train flew through a small station without stopping, and I tried and failed to read the platform sign. I had no idea whereabouts we were, just that we'd been travelling a long time, and the end of the journey couldn't come soon enough.

I missed Emily. I missed Oscar. I'd missed the weekend's marine rescue training. And I'd dragged Emily with me, which meant she'd missed it too. My shoulders drew up, and I tucked my elbows into my sides. I missed Murph and David. David, who

I'd found attractive until I met Adam, the Coastguard man. Adam, who I'd found attractive until I met Karam, the paramedic.

Why was I so attracted to emergency service workers? Was it because I was one myself now? My old life as Monty Jones' arm candy seemed a distant memory. This trip to the North, especially once Emily departed, and I was alone, had taught me one thing.

Home was where the heart was. Home wasn't London, where I'd lived almost all my life, a meaningless existence of expensive, single-use clothes, red carpets, two-faced acquaintances and fashion magazine interviews. Home was Redcliff, among my new community; my new friends, where I was valued for my personality and my contribution to society, not my looks and how much flesh my dress revealed.

Redcliff-upon-Sea.

Home.

This train was taking me home.

The view blackened, and the noise of the train's motion changed as we echoed through a narrow tunnel. I returned to thinking about the case at hand.

Inspector Creaser's words entered my mind. *"Who d'you think you are? Miss Marple?"*

Maybe I fancied myself as a modern-day Miss Marple. But no one was investigating Mary's murder except me. No one seemed to think it *was* murder. And what about this latest twist? Nora, Mary's bridesmaid, killed by Patrick's best man. Why?

Another 'why?'

And what possible connection could there be between Nora's death and Mary's death? None of this would bring closure to John Smith, grieving for his sister and the lost life he'd had without her.

I sat up and fluffed my hair. I knew I'd missed something. Some big clue had eluded me, seemingly innocuous, yet vitally important.

Maybe Nora and the best man knew each other in some unrelated way? They lived in neighbouring streets, after all, although they moved in completely different circles. Nora was a decent person, unknown to the police. The best man, by all accounts, had a substantial prison record. What possible connection could their lives have had, apart from that one meeting at the wedding forty-seven years ago?

Why?

Why? Why? Why?

I folded my arms on the table between the seats, laid my head on them and fell asleep.

Emily met me at Redcliff station. I rushed off the train, picked her up and spun her around as if we were long-lost lovers reunited after years apart, rather than friends who hadn't seen each other for two days.

"What's all this about?" she asked, wriggling out of my grip and straightening her clothes. "Are you feeling all right, Shiraz?"

"I've missed you; that's all. I've missed our banter and our funny chats. Milltown's a lonely place when you've no one to share it with."

"Right. I've missed you too, I suppose. I hadn't thought about it much. I've been so busy in the café, making up for my lost weekend. Oh. What did you do to your face?" She reached up to touch my graze, and I withdrew.

"It's nothing. I, um, fell off a train."

"You fell off a train? That's not nothing. Why didn't you tell me?"

I squeezed her shoulder. "Sorry. And thank you for coming with me. I wish you'd been able to stay longer."

Even though it was seven o'clock in the evening and dark, I forgave her for removing the convertible roof of her Morris Minor. I'd left the rain behind somewhere in the middle of my journey, and the temperature was bearable if I wore my beanie hat.

"What's the news?" I asked Emily, as she released the handbrake. "Did you find John Smith? Did you discover why he discharged himself?"

"No. Although, to be honest, I haven't looked for him."

"Did anyone at the hospital say anything? Like where he was going, or why? I don't understand why he'd abscond from there; he's homeless, and that place provided him with shelter, a bed and three meals a day. You're sure he discharged himself? They didn't kick him out?"

"He definitely discharged himself; I know the nurse on duty. Apparently, the police had asked her to take some of his blood for a DNA test, so they could compare it with a sample from Mary's body to see if they were related."

"That was my idea. Oscar must've suggested it."

"But the nurse told me he'd refused the test. He said, if he sees a needle, he faints."

"I know that's not true. While I visited him at the hospital last week, they took some blood for tests, and he didn't object."

"Ooh, Shiraz, is this a clue? The only reason someone would refuse a DNA test is because they're not who they say they are, right?"

"Right. Or maybe they know the skeleton isn't who we think it is? Either way, John Smith knows more than he's told us."

"How can we ask him? He's disappeared."

"Have you checked Golden Beach?"

"Are you serious? You think he might've swapped his comfortable, safe hospital bed for the freezing cold of Golden Beach, after we'd rescued him twice from there, and he'd been hospitalised with hypothermia?"

"Yep. I'll bet that's where he's gone. Can we divert and take a look?"

"But it's dark."

"And?"

"Shiraz, I'm not driving this little old car along that gravel track up to the clifftop car park at night. How will you see if he's on the beach? D'you have infra-red vision among your many other qualities?"

I laughed. "No. But he'll probably have lit another fire. At least let's go up there and see if there's anything burning on the beach."

Emily stopped the car at the side of the road and banged the steering wheel. "Shiraz, please. Because of you and your wild duck chases…,"

"Goose."

Emily huffed. "…your wild goose chases, I've fallen down a landslip, come face to face with a skeleton and spent a weekend jaunting around some factory town in the North when I should be staying right here, looking after my business and cuddling up on the sofa with Boots." She appeared ready to burst into tears. "And now, at 7:30 in the evening, you want me to drive my car up an unlit, rough track along a cliff edge to find some ungrateful vagrant who's absconded from his nice, warm hospital bed and is voluntarily sleeping on a deserted beach. He's spent one night there already; another won't harm."

"If he's spent one freezing night there already, a second could kill him."

Emily clasped her hands around the back of her neck and crashed her forehead on the steering wheel. "Right now, Shiraz Jones, I could kill you. All right. We'll drive up there. But even if we see a fire burning on the beach below, we're going to call the authorities. The Coastguard. Or the police. We're not going to investigate it ourselves. Got it?"

I grinned and nodded meekly. "Got it. Oh, and Emily." I held her arm. "Thank you. I've so missed your company."

"Ppff. Missed my unwilling cooperation, more like." She swung the wheel, and we headed through Redcliff's dark, deserted streets towards the clifftop road.

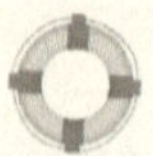

CHAPTER THIRTY

Gravel crunched under the Morris Minor's tyres as Emily steered gingerly up the track towards the Golden Beach clifftop car park. The car's headlights weren't the bright beams modern vehicles boasted, and Emily peered over the steering wheel as their dim, yellow glow illuminated the ground a few feet in front of us. We stopped once they lit up the wooden fence at the edge of the car park.

"People will wonder what we're doing, coming here after dark," said Emily.

I giggled. "They'll think we're a pair of lovers, looking for some nighttime privacy."

"Shiraz, don't be inappropriate."

I could sense her blush, even though I couldn't see her face.

"You can't see the beach from here," I said. "We'll have to walk up the path. Did you bring a torch?"

"Of course I didn't. I left home tonight to collect you from the railway station. Why would I have brought a torch?"

"Okay, shine the car headlights this way. We'll walk as far as we can until the beam runs out."

Emily turned the lights on, and we followed their path until we could see their glow behind us, and blackness in front.

"I can see the beach," I said.

"How?"

"Look." I pointed in the direction of crashing surf. "You can make out the white line where the waves are breaking. In the starlight."

"Can you see a fire?"

"No. But I can't see the whole beach from here. The part under the cliffs is hidden."

"I absolutely draw the line at walking up to the cliff edge in the dark. Sorry, Shiraz. That would be stupid."

"Yes. I suppose you're right." I stood on the path, stared downwards and tried to imagine what it must be like, being alone down there with my memories, after dark, without even my dog for company. The night was unusually mild for early spring, warmer than when we'd rescued John the previous week, and I desperately hoped he was safe.

"He's not there, Shiraz. Come on, let's go home. I'll make cheese and Marmite toasted sandwiches." Emily turned away and walked back to the car.

I stared into the black and listened to the waves' rhythmic pounding.

Are you down there, John? What are you running from? What secret are you hiding?

I took one last look at where the surf broke, turned away and followed Emily back to the car.

My head rested in my hands as I sat at a table in the Wicked Whelk café the following morning. Oscar faced me, while Emily cleared up in the kitchen.

"Stop worrying, Shiraz," he said. "Every mystery has low points, where nothing seems to make sense, and all the clues point nowhere. In my experience, the best way to resolve this is to write down everything you know and run it past someone else. Me, for instance." He rubbed his hands together, and the gleam in his eyes betrayed his eagerness to play detective again in his retirement. "Emily," he called, "could you pass me some paper and a pen?"

Emily brought over a pad headed, 'Things to do today'. She departed to continue cleaning.

"Okay. We have five deaths," I said.

"An epidemic," called Emily from behind the counter.

I ignored her and held up my splayed fingers to tick off the victims. "First, Mary Smith. Poisoned and killed in a landslide, while seated in the passenger seat of a blue Triumph Spitfire, registration number J-O-Y 42. The same vehicle used in a wedding at…"

"Hang on, hang on," said Oscar. "I can't write that fast."

"Sorry, if I don't pour it out quickly, I'll forget."

"Okay, ready."

"The car was used at the wedding of Mary to Patrick Hebblethwaite, in Milltown."

I paused and allowed Oscar to catch up.

"The second deaths were Patrick Hebblethwaite's parents, both from causes unknown, both on the same day, 2nd April, six weeks after the incident which claimed Mary's life."

Oscar scribbled.

"Then, a few weeks after that, in May, Patrick Hebblethwaite killed himself. We know, as it was reported in the local newspaper. That's the fourth death."

Emily shoved a plateful of squashed fruit buns in front of us. "I can't sell these. I accidentally rested a tray of pies on top of them. But they're fine for us to eat.

I selected a bun and absent-mindedly picked black, squidgy currants out of it. "And finally, forty-seven years later, we have the death of Nora Stubbins, an event which would appear to be wholly unconnected to the others, save for the fact that the murderer and the victim were both guests at Mary and Patrick's wedding."

Oscar scrawled, then laid down his pen and clasped his hands together. "How many of these deaths are under investigation?"

"Only one that I know of. Nora's."

"We have one death in Golden Beach, and four in, or near, Milltown. What did the police there say?"

"The detective wouldn't tell me anything. He played it close to his chest, drawing as much out of me as he could, while giving away minimal information."

"Clever man," said Oscar. "I'd have done the same."

"A young constable told me Patrick Hebblethwaite had killed himself but, as that information was in the newspapers, it's not as if she was betraying secrets."

"And they have Nora's murderer in custody? Who also happens to be Mary and Patrick's best man from decades ago." Oscar rubbed his flat palms together. "Coincidences, coincidences." He pursed his lips, then cleared his throat. "There are several people in this mix who may hold the key to how it all fits together, and all but two of them are dead."

"Two of them?" asked Emily.

"This best man, who the Milltown police have in custody, and the scruffy guy whose dog is still busy destroying my tomato plants."

"John Smith. Mary's brother."

"We don't know for certain he's her brother," Emily called from the kitchen. "He refused the DNA test, remember?"

"I wouldn't read too much into that," said Oscar. "People on the margins of society who've lived a life in mistrust of the law don't like giving up their fingerprints, let alone their DNA. The police can't force him to comply, as he hasn't committed a crime."

"He told me he's committed plenty of crimes," I said. "Surely they'd have his DNA on file, anyway?"

"You may well be right," said Oscar. "Okay, here's what we'll do. I'll make some discreet inquiries about this character the police in Milltown have in custody."

"How?" I shrugged. "They wouldn't tell me anything."

"Leave that to me. Then if you two could talk to John Smith?"

"I tried to last night. He ran away from the hospital," said Emily. "Discharged himself."

Oscar drummed his fingers on the table. "He was in there for hypothermia, right? He could've simply been feeling better?"

"He also has terminal cancer," said Emily, "and he coughs persistently." She huffed. "Shiraz dragged me up to the cliffs above Golden Beach in the middle of the night to see if this chap was down there again."

"It wasn't the middle of the night," I said. "It was 7:30."

"Whenever. It was pitch black and scary. We couldn't see a thing."

"Please have another look for him," said Oscar. "I feel like he's either not told us the truth, or he's withholding something. Plus, lovable rogue that it is, I need to give his dog back before it completely wrecks my vegetable garden."

"The search for John Smith'll have to wait for now," said Emily to me. "We have marine rescue night training at 6:00 p.m."

I tilted my head and frowned.

"Don't tell me you've forgotten, Shiraz? You were so excited when Murph said we'd be going out on the boat in the dark."

"Sorry, I thought that was at the weekend. But now I know it's this evening; it's given me an idea."

"Shiraz, don't be ridiculous." Murph's veins on his arms tensioned as he gesticulated. "What on earth is this chap doing back on Golden Beach? We've rescued him from there twice; the second time he was treated for hypothermia, and my understanding is, he's been admitted to the hospital."

"He discharged himself. And he's not definitely back on Golden Beach. I only wondered if we could search there during this evening's night training. You could make it an exercise. Combing Golden Beach shoreline for a missing person."

Murph huffed. "Flustering fathometers. The amount of combing we've given Golden Beach's shoreline recently; we'll be better practised at it than anything else we train for. I did have a fire refresher in mind, as we're still rather rusty about that, aren't we? We'll sweep past and look at Golden Beach while we're out. But your chap better not be there again. I may not be so nice to him this time."

I bristled at the reference to John Smith being 'my chap' but decided not to react to Murph's comment.

The sun had long set by the time we'd kitted up in our waterproofs, checked everything was present and working on the rescue boat and headed out of Redcliff Harbour. A blanket of cloud meant no stars shone above the flattest calm I'd ever experienced. The air temperature was close to freezing, and I touched the tip of my nose to ensure it was still there. Scattered snowflakes settled on the boat's surfaces and immediately melted.

"Wind speed force zero on the Beaufort scale," said Frances, the qualified crew on this evening's shift. "Smoke rises vertically."

"I love the snow," said Emily. "It reminds me of the exciting nights before Christmas and going to the Marine Rescue Christmas Barn Dance. I can't wait for this year's one."

I laughed. "Christmas is nine months away."

"You'll see what I mean, Shiraz. The best night of the year in Redcliff."

The only ripples on the water were the triangle of our boat's wake, which fanned out behind us and disturbed the perfect mirror of the sea. Murph pushed the throttles forward, the vessel picked up speed, and we spoilt the surface of the smoothest water ever. We rounded the promontory to the east of Redcliff and entered the wide bay of Golden Beach.

"Perishing picaroons," exclaimed Murph. "You were right. A fire, right at the bottom of the landslip. Looks like your friend's made another appearance."

We ploughed through the water and came to a spectacular stop directly in front of the flames. The boat's spotlight revealed a figure sitting next to it, huddled under a grey blanket. If I hadn't known who I was looking at, I would've thought they were an isolated rock.

Frances pointed at the smouldering embers as the searchlight illuminated the scene. "A perfect demonstration. Force zero. Smoke rises vertically."

"Never mind that," said Murph. "Hop over the side, and let's have a third and final chat with him."

The snow fell more heavily as Frances waded ashore by herself. I wasn't needed this time to bring Rebel, as he was still busy creating his own landslips among Oscar's tomatoes. She returned, carrying John Smith in her arms exactly as David had.

But this time was different. John Smith wasn't coughing.

"Shiraz," Frances yelled as she waded. "Radio Coastguard Headland Bay. Tell them to call an ambulance to meet us at Redcliff Harbour immediately. We have an unconscious casualty."

CHAPTER THIRTY-ONE

The rescue vessel skimmed across the flat water with the engines screaming at full throttle. Emily, Frances and I lay alongside John Smith, whose breathing was so shallow I repeatedly held my cheek to his mouth as I'd been taught, to ensure it hadn't stopped altogether. Our body heat, a thermal head cowl and the boat's silver foil survival blanket made the only difference between him living and freezing to death. He'd wrapped himself in two blankets he'd pinched from the hospital but, on that windswept, snowy beach, they weren't offering sufficient warmth for his bony body. Despite the dark, he retained his sunglasses.

"How long did the ambulance say they'd be?" asked Frances.

I checked my watch. "Ten minutes. Maybe less."

"They'd better reach Redcliff before us," yelled Murph, as he attempted to shove the throttles so far forward they risked snapping off. We swept into Redcliff Harbour, ignoring the five knot speed limit, and Frances deftly tied fenders and ropes as we touched the dock.

The ambulance approached simultaneously with blue lights flashing, and it stopped alongside the boat. Emily and I hugged John Smith tightly, and I was thankful the hospital had bathed him, and he didn't smell quite so bad.

Two paramedics pulled a stretcher from the rear of the ambulance and lifted our casualty onto it. I looked into the face of one, and my heart skipped briefly as I met eyes with Karam. We had no time to renew our acquaintance, as he and his colleague wrapped John Smith in thermal coverings and strapped an oxygen mask to his face.

"Are any of you accompanying the casualty?" asked Karam. "The hospital staff may have questions for first responders."

"I will," I said, and clambered into the back of the ambulance, where Karam clipped a monitor onto John's finger and lifted his sunglasses away from his face to shine a small torch into his eyes. The other paramedic slammed the doors, and I just had time to strap on a seatbelt before we lurched away.

Karam impressed me by being able to perform checks on John while asking me questions.

"Where did you find him?"

"On Golden Beach. He'd lit a fire and gone to sleep."

"Same place as last time. But on this occasion, he's in a much worse condition. Not surprising, given the air temperature tonight. Remind me of his name?"

"John Smith. And you should also be aware he has terminal cancer. I discovered that when I visited him during his last hospital stay."

Karam made notes on an iPad. "He's not going to prolong his life by continually trying to freeze himself to death, is he?"

I braced myself, as the ambulance turned a corner. The blue flashing light reflected eerily from the hedgerows as we sped through the country lanes. "Is he going to die?" I inquired, and immediately castigated myself for asking such a pointless, unanswerable question.

Karam raised his eyebrows at me. "His temperature's rising, but it's still in the range for severe hypothermia. If you hadn't found him when you did, he wouldn't have survived the night. He might not yet."

"Here," called the other paramedic from the driver's seat, as bright lights illuminated Redcliff and Alnchurch hospital's Accident and Emergency department. She parked directly outside the entrance, where three medical staff waited.

As soon as the ambulance's rear doors opened, the two paramedics removed John's stretcher, and medical staff wheeled it into the hospital. Karam updated them as we marched together down a starkly lit corridor, the stretcher trundling between us. "This is John Smith, sixty-four years old, removed from Golden Beach thirty minutes ago by Redcliff Marine Rescue, unconscious and severely hypothermic. Body temperature when handed to us: 28 degrees. Temperature now: 30 degrees. First aid given: thermal coverings applied, oxygen via face mask. This lady's an employee of Marine Rescue and was first responder on scene. Did you give him any other medical treatment I haven't mentioned?"

I shook my head, in awe at his professionalism. The cavalcade paused, and I looked on as the hospital staff transferred John onto a wheeled bed.

"You're welcome to wait for me," said Karam. "I'll complete handover and find you shortly."

I strolled back towards the hospital entrance, begging whatever higher being John Smith believed in to let him live, at least until I'd had another chance to talk with him. My eyes watered as I realised Rebel had no idea his owner was in hospital on death's door, and he might never see him again.

I sat on the end of a row of chairs, hugged myself and wept.

"Are you okay? D'you want to talk?" Karam crouched in front of me. I lifted my head, and his face came into focus through my tears. I wiped a hand over my eyes, which probably resulted in my makeup forming black streaks across my cheeks.

"Hi." I gave him a watery smile. "Sorry; John Smith's really got to me. He's had such a tragic life, all the way back to boyhood, and he probably won't live much longer. Sixty-four years, and nothing to show for it. Nothing. Will he be okay?"

Karam remained silent for a moment. "It's hard to tell. His temperature's dangerously low. And you mentioned he had other serious medical conditions. He's been transferred to intensive care, so that's the best place if he's going to recover." He sat next to me and clasped his hands together on his legs. "Shiraz. It is Shiraz, isn't it?"

"Yes." My heart fluttered as he spoke my name.

"In our job, we see so many lost souls. People like John Smith, who've never had the opportunities you and I have had. Never been able to gain a proper education or hold down anything that could be considered a career. I'm not only talking about those on the margins of society; I also mean honest, upstanding people who, for whatever reason, haven't been able to reach their full potential. Women who've spent their entire lives caring for their husbands and children, and then find themselves living alone in their later years, with no purpose and no passion. Men who've passed their whole existence living with their divorced mothers and wake up one day after Mum's died to discover they're fifty-eight years old, and they've achieved nothing. Soldiers who've returned from war to find nobody cares about what they've seen or done, and the evening's fatuous television offering is more riveting to their family than their tales of heroism. So many lost souls."

"This is the first one I've encountered. Does it get easier?"

"You build walls. Mental walls between your private life and your professional one. But some walls are porous. Some people you never forget."

"Do you have family, Karam?"

"I have a wife in Punjab."

My heart stopped, and I forgot to breathe.

"But she is my wife in name only."

I puffed out and smiled, then hoped he hadn't noticed my relief.

"She came from the Punjab to marry me; she had never been away from home before. I tried to help her settle in for the sake of our marriage, but life here wasn't easy for her. She struggled to make friends, missed her family and returned to India within a year."

I wondered how anyone could not want to stay married to a handsome, kind, intelligent, caring man like Karam. And I decided to bite the bullet.

"Karam, would you like to have dinner with me?"

His eyes opened wide, and he hesitated. I wondered if he'd ever had a girl ask him out. Especially one from a very different background.

"As friends and colleagues," I said, backpedalling slightly, but hopefully not too much. "We can talk about life as emergency service workers."

"It's been a long time since I went for dinner with anyone." He smiled. "I must warn you; I'm a vegetarian."

Of course you are.

"How about Saturday evening?" I asked. "We could go to the Tandoori Cottage here in Alnchurch. I've seen their menu, and I know they have a choice of vegetarian dishes. Shall I book for seven o'clock?"

"It sounds enticing. I would like that."

I smiled at him, desperately attempting to hide any outward signs of my heart bouncing between my belly button and my throat. "It's a date."

Karam's colleague approached us, her pager sounding from her hip. "Time to go. Next one."

We stood, and Karam and I shook hands awkwardly. I would've preferred to give him a movie star embrace as the closing credits played to a Bollywood blockbuster, but that would have to wait.

"Until next Saturday," he said, and they marched out to the ambulance.

I watched them leave, then reached for my phone and dialled. "Hi, Emily. Could you collect me from the hospital, please? I've good news and bad news."

I fiddled with my phone while I waited for Emily. I wondered if I could find a social media profile for Karam but, without his surname, my efforts were wasted.

Knowing John Smith was in the same building as me, unconscious and in intensive care, made me feel helpless. I'd tried to assist him and failed. And whatever secrets he may've been keeping to himself might now never be revealed. I screwed my eyes up, as Emily's Morris Minor swung around to the hospital entrance.

"Have you been crying?" she asked, as I opened the passenger door.

"I may have shed a tear, yes."

"More than one tear. Your mascara pattern looks like Rambo's camouflage."

I pulled down the passenger sun visor and inspected my reflection. I hardly recognised myself, with puffy eyes and black smudges smeared everywhere.

No wonder Karam hesitated when I asked him out.

"Good news and bad news?" prompted Emily, as we drove away.

"Which d'you want first?"

"Bad news, please. I'll need the good news after it to cheer me up."

"John Smith might not make it. His body temperature's dangerously low and, coupled with his other conditions, he's in a bad way. He's unconscious and in intensive care."

"I'm sorry for him. I've no idea what prompted him to keep returning to Golden Beach, but no one deserves to die from cold in this day and age. Um, what's the good news?"

I grinned, reached over and squeezed her leg. "I've got a date with Karam."

"Seriously?" Emily turned to me, wide eyed. "This John Smith chap's almost taken his last breath, and you're chatting up the paramedics. You, Shiraz Jones, are too much. That's plain callous."

I held up my palms towards her. "It wasn't like that. I needed comforting words after we'd delivered John into the care of the hospital staff. The whole situation left me feeling emotional. Karam's a lovely, caring guy and, um, I quite like him."

"And the fact that he has those dark, exotic, film-star looks has nothing to do with it?"

I nudged her. "Maybe. We're only going out as friends and fellow emergency service workers."

"Right. When and where is this date?"

"Saturday evening at the Tandoori Cottage, near the hospital. I don't suppose you could give me a lift, could you?"

Emily and I sat at her dining table the following evening, sharing crispy takeaway cod and chips. Boots lay at the other end of the table, eyeing the steaming, white, flaky fish. Occasionally, a hopeful ginger paw would extend towards the wrapping, and Emily would gently push it back.

"Now what, Shiraz?" She topped up my wine. "Where do we go from here?"

"I don't know. We'll get nothing out of John Smith. Even if he regains consciousness, I don't feel right marching up to his hospital bed and quizzing him about people from decades ago who he's probably forgotten. He was seventeen at the time of Mary's wedding. I can't imagine he'd have any information about a relationship between Nora and the best man." I thumped the table, which made Boots jump off and hide in the corner, staring at us. "I know I've missed something. A clue, staring me in the face. I wonder if Oscar had any luck with his inquiries."

"Time to find out," said Emily, as three loud raps came from the front door.

"Hi Oscar," I said, as his trilby hat appeared up the stairs. "I'm so pleased to see you. Did you have any luck with the Milltown constabulary?"

"All in good time," said Oscar. "Let me take off my coat first." He hung up his rain jacket and sat opposite me while Emily fetched a third wine glass and poured him a drink.

"I know that look," I said, leaning towards him. "You've found something out, haven't you?"

"I may have." Oscar wiggled his fingers at me like a magician preparing to reveal a rabbit.

Emily joined us. "Spill the beans, then. What've you got?"

"This was a tough task you set me. Very tough. I'm a civilian now, and I can't go ringing up a police force in another part of the country and asking them to share information with me, as I could've done when I was in the job."

"Privacy laws?" I said. "I understand."

"But we badly need to discover what the man accused of Nora Stubbins' murder had to say, don't we? It could be crucial to tie up the loose ends of Mary Smith's death."

"Yes. If only we were flies on the wall of the Milltown police station."

Oscar produced a folded sheaf of paper from his jacket pocket and smoothed it out on the table. "And given that I'm no longer a serving policeman, what I have here clearly isn't a transcript of the Milltown police interview with the suspect, is it?"

"Oscar! How on earth? How did you come by that?"

Oscar closed his eyes, grinned and shrugged. "I'm not the only one with friends in the North. Don't ask too many questions, and you won't be told too many lies."

"Come on," said Emily. "What does it say?"

Oscar held the pages up in front of him. "D'you want me to read it verbatim, or summarise it in my own words?"

I leant to peer at the top sheet and noticed it was written like a play, with a new line for each character. "In your own words, I think. If we need more details, you can elaborate."

"Okay. Here we go. It's a full confession. Nora's murderer, the best man, whose name we now know to be Ernest, or Ernie Groucher, is a career criminal. A violent man, who seems to have no scruples when it comes to threatening or injuring. He's spent most of his adult life in prison, and was last released at the age of 67, four years ago. He'd never been accused or convicted of murder, though. Armed robbery, yes. Actual bodily harm, yes. Threats with intent to kill, definitely. He maintains he didn't mean to kill Nora. He said he entered her house to give her a warning, but she wouldn't stop screaming at him. He wrapped his hands around her throat to frighten her into being quiet, but he didn't realise his own strength, and she slumped to the floor. At that point, he ran off."

"That would've been when the neighbour saw him." I rubbed my chin. "You said he came to give her a warning?"

"He told the police he'd received a call from an old underworld friend, and it seems he was in debt to this chap for some past favour. Honour amongst thieves, you might say. The caller asked him to visit Nora, and to warn her not to talk to anybody about any events in the past. If anyone came to see her asking about anything from a long time ago, she was not to give them any information. If she did, her life would be under threat."

"Who was the old underworld friend who called him?"

"This is where it gets weird, given what we know. He said the phone call came from Patrick Hebblethwaite."

CHAPTER THIRTY-TWO

I threw my hands in the air. "He's wrong. Patrick Hebblethwaite can't have called Ernie Groucher. He killed himself forty-seven years ago."

"Exactly my thoughts," said Oscar. "Anyway, this Detective Inspector Creaser teased more information out of him. I'm guessing he had in mind the information you gave him, Shiraz, and he wanted to find out if Ernie was responsible for Mary's death, too. And the story he told was quite extraordinary."

I sat back and sipped my wine. Boots had successfully stolen a piece of leftover fish and crunched the batter on the floor. Oscar tapped his papers as if he were about to deliver a speech.

"Patrick Hebblethwaite was a wicked, violent man. Probably worse than this Ernie character. But, unlike Ernie, Patrick was smart and devious, and he'd stayed off the police radar by various subterfuges. His downfall was an eye for the ladies. He'd do anything for a good-looking girl. It seems poor Mary was an attractive, fresh-faced young lass, and she caught Patrick's attention. We know, Shiraz, from what you found out, that

Mary was in dire financial straits after the deaths of her mother and father. Along comes this dapper, flash character with a convertible sports car and an aura of wealth around him. He whisks her off her feet, much to the disappointment of his Catholic parents."

Oscar looked up over the papers. "If only she'd known, being of a different belief was the least of Mary's problems." He sipped his wine and continued. "Patrick's legitimate job was as a hospital porter in Milltown, but he was involved in many criminal rackets with Ernie, and he'd been caught stealing drugs from the hospital pharmacy. The hospital wanted to avoid a scandal, so they didn't call the police; they fired him."

"Ernie told the police all of this?"

"He did. Personally, I reckon the detective would've thought it was all a big story to deflect attention from Ernie's own crimes. Shall I go on?"

"Please do," I said. "It's fascinating."

"Patrick and Mary married at Milltown registry office. Patrick got himself a new job at Redcliff and Alnchurch Hospital, far enough away for his reputation not to follow him. He brought Mary to live down here at a vacant holiday house they rented in Golden Beach. Ernie remembered him giving Mary's brother some cash at the wedding and saying they'd send for him as soon as they had somewhere to live."

"Poor John," I said. "He never saw his sister again."

"Right," said Oscar. "And here's where we fill in some gaps. Some weeks later, Patrick came knocking at Ernie's door."

"So he did return to Milltown? Nora was right."

"Indeed. Ernie said Patrick sat down in his front room and, as cool as a cucumber, told him he'd killed her."

"Killed Mary?"

"Correct. Apparently, she hated living in Golden Beach, resented Patrick for never bringing her brother to live with them like he said he would, missed her life in the North and her best friend Nora, and wanted to go home. He told Ernie her demands had driven them apart, wrecked the marriage; he'd even started a relationship with another woman, a nurse who worked at the hospital here. Eventually, Mary made his life hell to the point where, one night, in a vicious rage, he grabbed her roughly and broke her neck."

I covered my mouth. "Wow. Poor girl. Eighteen years old, and violently murdered by her new husband. Her dreams of a new life shattered. It doesn't matter how angry and bitter she was towards him, nothing excuses that. And you can totally understand her rage; he'd dragged her away from her brother and friends on false pretences to a place where she knew no one."

Emily leant forward. "What about the poison? The overdose of the Melar-whatever?"

Oscar nodded. "This is where the story gets a little fuzzy. He didn't tell Ernie anything else about the murder, so we can only assume these events happened close to the night of the great storm. Patrick must've obtained the Melarsoprol somehow, administered it to Mary to make her death look like a medical accident, put Mary in the car, shoved it over the cliff in all the confusion that night, and then made a run for it, in the hope the local emergency services believed she was a victim of the power of nature."

"And there the car lay buried," I said, "for forty-seven years, until this month's new landslip uncovered it."

"Yep," said Emily. "And Rebel, the dog, who belonged to John Smith, led you to his sister's body."

"Incredible. What a coincidence."

"The tale doesn't end there," said Oscar. "Ernie went on to say he gave Patrick Hebblethwaite shelter to keep him hidden from the authorities, while he grew a beard, dyed his hair and generally changed his appearance. Apparently, he went out to the supermarket once, when Ernie hadn't brought enough food home for them both. Ernie hit him in a rage, because he could've been recognised, and then Ernie would be in trouble for harbouring a murderer."

"That'd be when Nora saw him and told the police."

"Yes. And Ernie said the police came around to his house after that, looking for Patrick. But they didn't check a dog kennel in the garden, where he was hiding. Subsequently, Patrick went missing again for two whole days. When he returned to Ernie's house, he'd changed his appearance even more, and Ernie didn't recognise him at first. He'd plastered dark makeup on his face, which, together with the beard, made him appear older than his years. Ernie understood Patrick's parents had passed away, and he'd inherited their remote farmhouse. He planned to live there and didn't need Ernie to hide him anymore."

"I think he killed them," said Emily.

"Very probably," said Oscar, "but we may never know that. Ernie then continued his career of unrelated crimes and prison sentences of various lengths, and that's where the story ends."

"At least we now know who murdered Mary," I said. "Although, we guessed that all along. But now we have a new mystery. Because if Patrick Hebblethwaite killed himself in 1976 while resisting arrest, how can he have instructed Ernie to visit Nora and threaten her this week?"

"Unfortunately," said Oscar, "this is where the trail goes cold. Ernie's testimony doesn't answer that question."

"Could Ernie have been simply lying about the phone call coming from Patrick Hebblethwaite?" asked Emily. "Maybe he murdered Nora for another reason, and this is all a big story to blame Nora's death on someone who's dead themselves?"

"Ernie confessed to killing Nora," I said. "I can't understand why he'd make up a story about someone he knew forty-seven years ago telling him to do it."

Oscar finished his wine. "On a related subject, Mary's funeral's being held tomorrow at 3:00 p.m. Here, at the Anglican church. The police couldn't trace any relatives apart from John Smith, who's unconscious in hospital, so it'll be a quiet affair."

"I'm going," I said, and I felt my eyes moisten. "It's the least I can do. That poor girl, murdered at eighteen, then spending forty-seven years buried in a landslip, and then to have no one at her funeral. Life's so unfair. Will you come with me, Emily?"

"Of course I will."

"We'll all go," said Oscar. "Mary deserves some respect before she's laid to rest."

"God of the orphan and the forgotten, remember your daughter Mary, and grant her shelter in your love. Welcome her into your kingdom, so that she may find rest at last. In the name of your Son, Jesus Christ our Lord."

The vicar stood in the centre of the aisle behind the coffin. I'd imagined Oscar, Emily and I would be the only mourners, but intrigue of the circumstances of Mary's death had attracted a crowd, and the church service was standing room only. I noticed Roy Bartlett snapping discreet photos, and I reckoned there'd be a front page article in the forthcoming edition of the *Headland Bay Times*. Bill Leonard nodded a greeting at me, sporting a crumpled suit which looked like it hadn't been worn in decades. The throng listened attentively as the priest murmured a sermon. She must've adapted a generic one, as no one here had known Mary, only her manner of death. Tears welled up as I realised she'd be forgotten as soon as this ceremony was over; the only person who'd grieve her was on death's door in Redcliff and Alnchurch Hospital. I'd visited John Smith that morning, and he hadn't regained consciousness.

The priest made a sign of the cross above the coffin. "Go forth upon your journey from this world, in the name of Jesus Christ, who suffered death for you. Aided by angels and archangels, may you dwell for evermore in the Father's house. Amen."

"Amen," we all echoed and, as organ music played, six people dressed in funeral company attire picked up Mary's coffin and carried it to a waiting hearse. Each member of the congregation turned to face it as it passed, and they bowed their heads.

As one of them inclined towards the coffin, I recognised her distinctive side profile.

"Oscar." I nudged him and whispered. "The woman in the blue coat? That's Violet Farmer, from the museum, isn't it?"

"Yes. Why?"

I whipped out my phone, scrolled to the photos I'd taken at Bill Leonard's house and enlarged one with my two forefingers. "What was her career before she volunteered there? She was a nurse, wasn't she?"

"I believe so. In the 1970s, at Redcliff and Alnchurch Hospital. Later on, I remember she had a job at Headland Bay library."

"Hmm. A nurse, then a librarian." I set my jaw and nodded. "Something's red-flagging in my mind. A vague hunch which may be completely wrong. But I need to have a quick word with her. We might be able to clear up one aspect of this mystery."

"Violet?" I tapped her on the shoulder.

She turned. "I'm sorry. Do I know you?"

"We have met before. I visited the museum asking about the photo of the couple missing in the landslip. Patrick and Mary Hebblethwaite."

"Hah! At least we know what happened to Mary now, don't we? Poor girl. What a terrible accident. Anyway, I can't stand here chatting all day. Things to do." She turned away from me and walked on.

I grabbed her arm. *Deep breath. You'd better be right about this.*

"Not so fast, Violet. You know more than you're telling about Patrick Hebblethwaite, don't you?"

She averted her eyes. "Sorry, my dear. I don't know what you mean."

"You were a nurse at Redcliff Hospital, weren't you?"

"Before I was married, yes." She stiffened. "What of it?"

"I think you were quite taken by a young, handsome hospital porter who'd moved from the North with his new wife."

"Wherever did you get that idea?"

Here we go, Shiraz. No going back.

"You told me you were at the landslip in your nurse's uniform. The newspaper reporter, Bill Leonard, caught a photo of you bandaging a man's shoulder. And the person you were attending to was Patrick Hebblethwaite, your lover, wasn't it? You knew all the time he'd survived the landslip, but his wife hadn't. And I think you know why she didn't. I think you, or he,

269

stole powerful drugs from the hospital and killed her with them. Something called Melarsoprol."

Phew. Now we find out if that entire statement was complete guesswork.

"I didn't kill anyone." Her voice was shaky, and she licked her lips repeatedly. "Mary didn't die from the Melarsoprol. She died from a broken neck."

Gotcha.

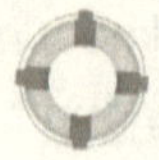

CHAPTER THIRTY-THREE

Violet gasped, her skin paled, and she covered her mouth.

"Broken neck, Violet?" I challenged her. "How did you know she had a broken neck before she was put in the car? Did you help put her in the car? Should I call the police and tell them to arrest you for murder? Or, at the very least, an accessory to murder?" I towered over her, while she stooped and glanced over both shoulders to see if anyone was listening. "And while you were working as Headland Bay librarian, you destroyed the evidence, didn't you? The microfilms from the *Redcliff and Golden Bay Herald* are missing from February 1976, complete with potentially incriminating photos. Why, Violet? What were you covering up?"

Her whole body began to tremble, and I grabbed her upper arm and steered her to a bench at the edge of the churchyard, where she sat and clawed her hands through her hair.

"I didn't kill Mary," she said, almost inaudibly. "That evil man Patrick Hebblethwaite took a fancy to me at work. I'll admit, I was charmed by his approaches, and we had a brief fling. He said he didn't get along with his wife, and he didn't want to stay with her, but I replied I wasn't interested in continuing a relationship with a married man. Then he began to talk about the bad things he'd done, how he'd hurt people in the past; I mean, physically hurt them, and I became very afraid of him."

I could see the fear on her face as she recalled the events.

"He blackmailed me into stealing the Melarsoprol. He told me if I didn't, he'd hurt me too. So I sneaked into the hospital pharmacy, took it and gave it to him in a little milk bottle along with a needle. Then there was that terrible night; no one of my age will ever forget it. I travelled to the Golden Beach settlement directly from my shift at the hospital. I was still wearing my uniform; oh, it was so cold; I stayed close to the fire. I took medical supplies with me; I knew they'd be needed. People lined up to have their wounds bandaged and ointment on their scrapes. Some poor people were beyond my level of medical capability."

She paused. "Then he turned up."

"He? Patrick Hebblethwaite?"

"Who else? He sat in front of me, bold as brass, and told me he'd sprained his shoulder, and he wanted me to bandage him up. I didn't dare show the other ladies who were helping that I knew him so, in my professional voice, I asked him where it hurt, and how he'd injured himself. His reply chilled me to the bone."

She paused and swallowed. I didn't fill her silence. *Thanks, Bill, for the old reporter's trick.*

"He told me he'd injured himself not being married anymore. He said he'd broken his wife's neck, then jabbed the Melarsoprol in her arm to make it look like an accidental overdose, or mis-prescription. Then he'd stuffed her body in the car; this was all during the night of that terrible storm, mind you, and he'd driven it to the edge of the cliff where the land had slid away, released the handbrake and hopped out. He told me he was returning to the North and, now he was a widower, there was nothing to stop me accompanying him and becoming his second wife."

She waited for my reaction, but I continued not filling silences.

Her voice lowered further. "He said, if I didn't go north with him, he'd frame me for her murder."

Her skin flushed during the conversation, and I hoped she wasn't going to faint.

"How was he planning to set you up?" I asked. "On what evidence?"

"He placed the little milk bottle on the table between us, looked me directly in the eyes and said, 'Violet, dearest, your fingerprints are all over this.'"

I gasped at the cunning of this evil man, as so many had described him. "What did you do, Violet? What did you reply?"

"What could I do? Here I was, surrounded by people, and this man had threatened to have me charged with the killing of his wife. I'd go to prison, and he'd literally get away with murder."

Her voice trembled as she relived the events of forty-seven years previously. She turned to me and set her jaw. "No way was I being framed for Mary's death. I said my father was a policeman, and he was right here, and I'd tell him what really happened. I pointed out Nicholas Murphy, the man organising everyone and making notes of names. Of course, he wasn't a policeman, nor was he my father, but Patrick Hebblethwaite wasn't to know that, was he? And Mr Murphy, with his suit and his clipboard, looked very official. I marched towards Nicholas, and when I turned around, Patrick Hebblethwaite had legged it up the road towards Redcliff-upon-Sea. And that was the last I ever saw of him, thank goodness. My whole body shook for hours afterwards; everyone assumed it was from the shock of seeing all the injuries from the landslip, but it wasn't. It was the after-effect of imagining life with him, or life in prison. Both would have been the end of my world. I swiped the milk bottle off the table and threw it into the fire, hoping that disposed of his evidence."

I sighed and shook my head.

"Do you believe me?" asked Violet. She reached out and gripped my forearm. "D'you believe I'm not a murderer? I may have behaved stupidly, as any love-struck young girl might, but I didn't kill Mary."

I held my head in my hands, then looked up. "I'm not sure what I would've done, had I been in your situation. I think you were brave, standing up to Patrick Hebblethwaite. Although, I do wish you'd gone to the police at the time."

"How could I? If I went to the police, even if I wasn't charged with murder, I'd have lost my job and my reputation for stealing the medicine. All my life I've lived with this over my head, Miss. I've thought of telling the authorities on so many occasions, but each time I've stopped myself. I'm sorry for Mary, but nothing I could've said would have brought her back. That man was evil, and I'm terrified of ever crossing paths with him."

"You won't see him again, Violet. He's been dead for decades."

"Has he?" She burst into tears and grabbed hold of me. "I wish I'd known. Good. He deserved it. Patrick Hebblethwaite was the devil in human form. I wouldn't be surprised to hear he'd murdered others." She wiped her eyes with a white handkerchief, and her hands trembled. "For the first time in years, I don't have to look twice at every stranger. I don't have to worry each time there's an unexpected knock at the door. My heart doesn't stop every time I see a police officer." She pressed her palms to her eyes. "Only a few weeks ago, I saw someone at the museum who looked like him, and I gasped and hid my face. All these decades later."

I sighed. "Violet, I won't tell anyone what you've intimated to me. I understand why you didn't inform the authorities in 1976. You've lived under a sentence of fear from that man your whole life. That sentence is over. But you must tell the authorities. It would be the correct thing to do. They need to know your information about who murdered Mary."

"You're right, Miss. I don't care anymore, now I know he can't hurt me."

Oscar and Bill Leonard chatted outside the church, as Emily met my eyes.

"Guess what? Bill and Oscar are becoming reacquainted."

"Hmph," said Oscar. "Doesn't mean we'll be best friends." He laughed. "It's good to see you, Bill. We must have a drink together and chat about the old times."

"Indeed," said Bill. "And what about this poor girl's death? I was right all along."

Oscar removed his trilby and scratched his head. "You were. And everyone thought your theory was ludicrous." He winked and grinned. "Like the rest of the rubbish you used to write."

"If you'd given me more information, I wouldn't have had to write so much rubbish, as you call it."

"Who were you talking to on that bench?" Emily asked me.

"Violet Farmer from the museum. I, err, suggested she could update her display; now we know what became of the young couple in the wedding photo."

"Such a tragedy," said Emily. "What a terrible thing to have happened to a teenage bride. And her brother doesn't even know she's dead."

"Oh?" said Bill. "Why not?"

"Because he's in hosp…"

"Bill, will you leave it?" interrupted Oscar. "You're almost eighty. Stop trying to sniff out stories everywhere. Take up lawn bowls or something."

"Sorry. Once a reporter, always a reporter."

We laughed.

"Are you ready for tonight, Shiraz?" asked Emily.

"Tonight? What's happening tonight?"

"Your date with the ambulance guy? The Indian chap with Bollywood movie star looks?"

"Gosh, is that tonight? No, I'm absolutely not ready. I only have four hours to choose an outfit, put on makeup, do my hair…"

"Come on," she said, rolling her eyes and laughing. "I'll give you a ride home so you can start applying the war paint."

CHAPTER THIRTY-FOUR

Karam sat opposite me at a table for two, fiddling with a gold ring on one of his immaculately manicured fingers. I'd never seen him out of his ambulance uniform, and I admired his dark-green shirt with twirly, gold, Indian symbols decorating the collar and cuffs. And his perfume smelt sooo exotic; musky and sultry. After only four changes of proposed outfit, Emily had helped me settle on a simple, sheer, cream, Christian Dior dress which reached below my knees. Not too revealing, in case that risked offending his culture. We were both significantly overdressed for Alnchurch's Tandoori Cottage, but I didn't care; excuses to put on my nicest attire were rarer now I lived in Redcliff-upon-Sea. Of course they were rarer; in my London life I'd changed clothes five times per day for different engagements. Karam's nerves were painfully obvious, so I reckoned the best mutual ground was to talk about our emergency services work.

"D'you have many jobs where you need to deal with unconscious patients?" I asked, wondering if that was a subject that should be discussed over dinner.

I rested my chin in my hands and fluttered my eyelashes at him, as I'd done so many times in city nightclubs with Monty. What a waste of time that was.

"Most of my work at this time of year's with the elderly," he replied. "Redcliff's a popular retirement area, so we see a lot of heart attacks or falls among the older population. Then, in the summer, it's people who've had too much to drink, or they've suffered an accident on the beach."

I nodded, smiled and didn't fill his silence. The waiter brought a starter of onion bhajis and placed them between us.

"Take the man from the other night," continued Karam, picking up the plate and offering it to me, which impressed me enormously. Monty would've grabbed the biggest one and left me with the dregs. "He was an unusual case. To be found in the same place, hypothermic, not once, but twice. D'you know if he regained consciousness?"

"He hadn't this morning, and the medical staff weren't hopeful. Having terminal cancer wouldn't have helped."

Karam took an onion bhaji and cut it. The two halves fell apart revealing the inside, and steam rose, mingled with the scent of aromatic spices. He smiled at me, and we lifted our glasses and clinked them together.

This is so romantic. The date's going well.

I smiled back and blushed.

His mouth formed a straight line. "That man, he wore sunglasses the entire time."

"Yes. I think he had a problem with his eyes which made him sensitive to light."

Karam rubbed his chin, and my chest tingled at the scratching sound his fingers made against his closely cropped, black beard.

He pursed his lips. "When I removed his sunglasses to shine the torch in his eyes and check if his pupils contracted, I noticed something odd. I've never seen it before. I learnt about at university, during my paramedicine degree. He was heterochromic."

"Heterochromic? Um, sorry, I'm not familiar with that term."

Goodness, he's so intelligent. What on earth does that mean?

"Less than one person in a hundred million are heterochromic. It means his eyes were different colours. One blue, and one green."

I dropped my fork. "Are you serious?" I pushed back my chair and jumped to my feet. "Karam, wait here. Order the main course. Order drinks. Whatever. I need to leave right now." I grabbed my coat, and to the amazement of my date, the wait staff and the other diners I sprinted out of the Tandoori Cottage and ran to the hospital as fast as my stiletto heels would carry me.

Running in stilettos resulted in one wrenched ankle. I definitely wasn't as fit as when I went to the gym every day. I bashed through the hospital's main entrance doors and pushed the elevator button multiple times to make it arrive faster.

Come on, come on.

The lift doors opened, I jumped in and waited for what seemed like hours for them to close. It ascended slowly and stopped to let people in and out on every floor. At the fourth level, I slipped through the doors before they'd opened fully, marched along the polished lino of the corridor and crashed open the double doors of the Intensive Care Unit. I strode to the nurse's station. "Hi," I puffed. "I'm here to inquire about John Smith." I clenched my teeth and muttered under my breath, "Also known as Patrick Hebblethwaite."

The ward sister exhaled loudly, reached forward and held my arm. "I'm so sorry, Madam. John Smith never regained consciousness. He passed away this afternoon."

CHAPTER THIRTY-FIVE

Two weeks later

Emily and I sat opposite Bill Leonard and Oscar in the Smuggler's Tavern on Redcliff's seafront. The permeating smell of real ale mixed with a background scent of salt water made a unique combination.

More comforting. More homely. More...Redcliff.

"This saga's an incredible story, Shiraz," said Bill. "I'm planning to write a book about the entire thing."

"Will I be in it?" asked Emily.

"Of course. You all will be. But I'll have to change your names. And maybe your occupations. You might need to become proper detectives in the book. I'm not sure how readers will react to marine rescue volunteers solving murders."

"You'd be surprised," I said. "All kinds of people investigate murders in books."

"Patrick Hebblethwaite was alive all along?" said Emily. "The cunning devil. He'd killed his wife, killed his parents and then somehow swapped identities with Mary's younger brother and framed him for their deaths. And the real John Smith, a mere teenager, shot himself in terror of being charged with crimes he didn't commit."

"All that story about the letter from his sister and coming back to Redcliff-upon-Sea to find her was rubbish," I said. "Patrick Hebblethwaite knew where Mary Smith was all the time, 'cos he'd put her there. And I inadvertently informed him we were headed to Milltown to investigate what happened to her."

"You believe the call to Ernie Groucher did come from him?" asked Oscar.

"Yep. After we'd departed for Milltown, he must've discharged himself and rung Ernie, instructing him to warn Nora not to speak to anyone about anything in the past. But Ernie was late with his threat, and we'd already met Nora, and she'd spilt the beans."

"Poor lady," said Emily, "getting mixed up in all this."

"The whole case is extraordinary," said Oscar. "I've discovered the Milltown Police had John Smith's body exhumed, and DNA tests proved his relationship to Mary. And that's why Patrick Hebblethwaite refused the test. It would've shown he wasn't John Smith; he wasn't Mary's brother at all. If you hadn't been out to dinner with that paramedic, Shiraz, no one would've ever known the truth."

Emily laughed. "Has Karam forgiven you for running out on him?"

"You should've seen the look of relief on his face when I returned fifteen minutes later." I chuckled at the memory and blushed. "He thought he'd said something to offend me, but then he realised I was bound to return as I'd forgotten my handbag."

Emily giggled. "Your expensive Hilda Panettone one?"

"Hilde Palladino, Emily. Hilde Palladino." I grinned and rubbed her arm.

"Whatever. I knew it was some Italian name."

"The one thing I can't work out in all this," I said, "is why Patrick Hebblethwaite returned to Redcliff at all. The only part of his story that was true was the lung cancer bit. He knew he hadn't long to live."

"We might never know," said Oscar. "Although, several times during my life as a serving policeman, I observed criminals return to the scene of their crime, often years later after they'd been released from their sentences. Maybe he came back to satisfy some morbid curiosity prior to his own death? He may have read about the new landslip and become concerned incriminating evidence had been exposed? Which, ironically, it had."

"He couldn't read," said Emily.

"John Smith couldn't read," I said. "Patrick Hebblethwaite may've been able to read perfectly well. I'm kicking myself for missing that clue earlier. He told me he couldn't understand the letter from his sister, but then later he said he read the newspaper article in Redcliff Museum."

Emily shrugged. "I'll always think of that scruffy man as John Smith. It's so confusing."

Bill leant across the table and grinned. "Once I publish the book, I'll be able to sell the movie rights for a fortune." He rubbed his hands together. "Not that I'm interested in the money, at my age. I'm glad to have been vindicated."

"If it's made into a movie," said Oscar, "who would play me? George Clooney, perhaps, or Sam Neill?"

"Ppff," said Bill. "They're both far too young. I reckon Mel Brooks. He's more your age."

"Mel Brooks?" Oscar feigned offence. "Isn't he almost 100? Anyway, I'm younger than you."

We all laughed.

"Oh, and one other thing," continued Oscar, "I'm happy to report Rebel's found a new home. I'd love to have kept him, but my vegetable garden wouldn't have survived. My eldest son's been looking for a dog, and he was delighted to take him. He was too good a pet for someone like Patrick Hebblethwaite. And he and Cadbury can have playdates together on the beach every day."

"How wonderful," said Emily.

I blew out my cheeks. "I'm relieved the truth was revealed. And it goes to show, if you study something for long enough, you'll work it out. All the clues added up in the end."

"Talking about studying," said Emily, "have you revised your fire training? Our final assessment's tomorrow."

"It is? Um, no. I haven't looked at my workbook at all. Could you give me a quick summary tonight?"

The marine rescue boat swung around the headland, past Golden Beach. I stared at the shingle as we zoomed by, half expecting to see smouldering embers with a figure crouching next to them, and a dog barking at me.

But the beach remained roped off and empty.

The landslip splayed out its giant, red fan. More earth had slid onto the beach in recent weeks, and I could see newly uprooted trees. But it no longer held its secret. No longer held a body. A body which had magnetised a killer and compelled him to revisit the scene of his crime again and again.

Why?

Was it guilt?

Was it, as Oscar had suggested, morbid curiosity or fear his crimes would be exposed?

Patrick Hebblethwaite's reasons for his actions were buried along with him, and his death completed a tragic series of lives coming to an end. So many, and all so senseless.

The rescue boat slowed to a stop, and Murph switched off the engines. He pulled out the marine rescue workbook and flopped it open somewhere near the centre.

I shook myself out of my depressing thoughts, turned to him, clenched my teeth and sucked in a breath.

"Ready, Shiraz?" he said. "Describe the fire triangle. What three elements must be present for a fire to exist?"

I turned to Emily and grinned. "Easy. I've plenty of experience with this subject."

Shiraz's adventures continue in book 4:
A Smuggler's Cave and a Watery Grave

SHIRAZ'S NEXT ADVENTURE

Hi, it's Simon.

Thank you so much for reading *A Landslide, a Bride and a Fatal Ride*, the third in my *Shiraz Jones Marine Rescue Mysteries* series.

 If you'd like to read more of Shiraz's adventures in Redcliff, why not:

Sign up for my newsletter at simonmichaelprior.com

Follow me on Amazon to be notified of new releases.

And please consider leaving a review to let other readers know how much you enjoyed it. A few words will suffice. Even if you didn't buy the book from Amazon, you can still leave a review there if you have a valid Amazon account. I read every one with interest and gratitude.

Now, if you wish, you could continue onto *Shiraz Jones Marine Rescue Mysteries* book four:

A Smuggler's Cave and a Watery Grave

Available from Amazon and all good bookshops.

MORE BOOKS BY SIMON

Available on Amazon and from all good bookshops

Shiraz Jones Marine Rescue Mysteries

A Murderous Clamour at Redcliff Manor
A Deadly Affair in the Pirate's Lair
A Landslide, a Bride and a Fatal Ride
A Smuggler's Cave and a Watery Grave
A Spook in the Dark at Alnchurch Park

Fun Travel Memoirs

The Coconut Wireless:
A Travel Adventure in Search of the Queen of Tonga
The Scenicland Radio:
A Travel Adventure in Search of the New Zealand Experience
The Pomegranate Busker:
A Travel Adventure in Search of New Zealand Rock Stardom
The Anticlockwise Proposal:
A Travel Adventure Around the World in Eighty Diamonds

A Capybara for Christmas:
European Travel, Japanese Adventure, Maximum Mayhem

Historical Memoirs

An Englishman in New York:
The Memoirs of John Miskin Prior 1948-1949

DISCLAIMER

A Landslide, a Bride and a Fatal Ride is a work of fiction, based on the experiences of Simon Michael Prior, a search-and-rescue skipper with one of the many volunteer marine rescue organisations seafarers depend on.

Although the book is set in England, the town of Redcliff-upon-Sea, the vanished settlement of Golden Beach and the surrounding locations are fictional. Hebble Bridge and Milltown are fictional locations. Montague Jones PR Ltd is a fictional company. *Red Carpet Superstars* magazine is a fictional publication. Which is a shame, as it sounds like a good read.

Names, characters, places and incidents are either products of the author's imagination or are used fictitiously. Any resemblance to actual events or locales or persons, living or dead, is entirely coincidental.

I had to say that.

ACKNOWLEDGEMENTS

This book wouldn't have been possible without the help of the following people: The wonderful beta readers: Alyson Sheldrake, Dawne Archer, Lisa Rose Wright, Louise Pierce, Rebecca Hislop and Val Poore; your feedback improved the final result so much.

Thank you to Nicholas Thresher for ensuring Shiraz's interactions with paramedics were medically accurate.

Thank you to Victoria Twead, Matthew J Holmes, Meg LaTorre, Craig Martelle, Angela Ackerman, Becca Puglisi, David Gaughran and Dave Chesson for informative courses, tips and useful tools.

Thank you to Jeff Bezos, for giving independent authors a platform on which to publish our writing.

And thank you so much to the skippers and crew of the AVCGA Volunteer Coastguard. I couldn't have done it without you.

ABOUT THE AUTHOR

Simon Michael Prior experiences constant adventures, hazards and exciting situations as a marine rescue skipper and a commander of rescue operations.

Although Simon is absolutely nothing like Murph, Redcliff Marine Rescue's burly, grumpy coxswain, many of the scenes in his stories are inspired by events he encounters during his duties.

Simon has also lived on two boats and sunk one of them; sold houses, street signs, Indian food and paper bags for a living; visited almost fifty countries and lived in three; qualified as a scuba diving instructor; nearly killed himself learning to wakeboard and built his own house without the benefit of an instruction manual.

He now lives in it by the sea with his wife and twin daughters, where he spends his time regurgitating his experiences on paper before he has so many more that he forgets them.

Website and newsletter sign up: simonmichaelprior.com
Email: simon@simonmichaelprior.com
Facebook: @simonmichaelprior
Instagram: @simonmichaelprior